"You really think we can make it work?"

"For a year." Paige had to make that point noticeably clear. And was suddenly way more nervous than she'd been since finding West Thomas in the foyer of Walter's home when she'd come to feed the dogs.

"Can we agree on the financial terms of the sale at the end of the year?"

With a slight head tilt, he studied her.

"I just don't want a dollar amount in the contract." Because she wasn't going to be put in a position where she was forced to take his money to buy her freedom. "You can say something like 'An amount not to exceed such and such amount of dollars,'" she quickly added. She could sign that.

Because she could be true to the agreement and still sell him her half of the estate for a dollar.

He named an amount that was far too generous. She didn't care. Her future request couldn't exceed that amount. Nothing said it couldn't be lower. And so she nodded.

He did, too.

Then he smiled at her.

Her body melted.

And she wondered what in the hell she'd let herself in for.

Dear Reader,

Welcome back to Sierra's Web—where friends who are experts in their fields work together to help people!

If you've ever seen me on social media, you'll know that I am a secret dog whisperer. My aunt once quipped that it's so me to remember a dog's name but not their owners' names. I chuckled at the time but have since been paying conscious attention to owners' names, too. In this case, this book, the people, Paige and Weston definitely have my full attention, and through them, I got to spend a lot of time with several very sweet, loving and loyal dogs. I can't wait for you to meet them all.

Sometimes in life we think we know best for others. West's uncle certainly thought he did. He overstepped his boundaries by a lot, and yet...I do love his heart. I love what he was trying to do. West and Paige most definitely didn't agree with me. I'm anxious to hear what you think...

You can find all of my socials, sales, news and giveaways, and a newsletter sign-up form at www.tarataylorquinn.com.

Tara Taylor Quinn

Reluctant Roommates

TARA TAYLOR QUINN

HARLEQUIN

SPECIAL
EDITION

HARLEQUIN®
SPECIAL EDITION™

Recycling programs for this product may not exist in your area.

ISBN-13: 978-1-335-40856-3

Reluctant Roommates

Copyright © 2022 by TTQ Books LLC

All rights reserved. No part of this book may be used or reproduced in any manner whatsoever without written permission except in the case of brief quotations embodied in critical articles and reviews.

This is a work of fiction. Names, characters, places and incidents are either the product of the author's imagination or are used fictitiously. Any resemblance to actual persons, living or dead, businesses, companies, events or locales is entirely coincidental.

For questions and comments about the quality of this book, please contact us at CustomerService@Harlequin.com.

Harlequin Enterprises ULC
22 Adelaide St. West, 41st Floor
Toronto, Ontario M5H 4E3, Canada
www.Harlequin.com

Printed in U.S.A.

Having written over ninety novels, **Tara Taylor Quinn** is a *USA TODAY* bestselling author with more than seven million copies sold. She is known for delivering intense, emotional fiction. Tara is a past president of Romance Writers of America and a seven-time RITA® Award finalist. She has also appeared on TV across the country, including *CBS Sunday Morning*. She supports the National Domestic Violence Hotline. If you need help, please contact 1-800-799-7233.

Books by Tara Taylor Quinn

Harlequin Special Edition

Sierra's Web

His Lost and Found Family
Reluctant Roommates

The Parent Portal

Having the Soldier's Baby
A Baby Affair
Her Motherhood Wish
A Mother's Secrets
The Child Who Changed Them
Their Second-Chance Baby
Her Christmas Future

The Daycare Chronicles

Her Lost and Found Baby
An Unexpected Christmas Baby
The Baby Arrangement

The Fortunes of Texas

Fortune's Christmas Baby

Visit the Author Profile page
at Harlequin.com for more titles.

To Taylor and Jerry: my office mates, my family members and my teachers of all the important things. I hope you've felt my love and adoration and that I've made your lives worth living.

Chapter One

Exhausted from the long drive, Weston Thomas was aggravated, to say the least, when he heard a key unlocking the front door of his deceased father's home. Walter Thomas, inventor, had attracted dreamers and free spirits his entire life. And in later years, gold-diggers and users, too. No telling who might have been given a key to his Georgia mansion.

Hands on the hips of his gray dress pants, Weston stood in the grand foyer, eyes steely, ready to defend his territory on that early Saturday morning. Top dead bolt undone. Handleset would be next. He watched for the inside lever to turn. The trespasser would make it no farther than one step in the door before being directed back out again, with the heavy wooden door at his or her back.

Being an accountant, and not a law enforcement officer, didn't mean a man couldn't be fierce and protect when the situation demanded. He had the height. Worked out. What smart person didn't want to stay healthy and able?

Metal against metal as the key slid into the lower lock.

He could just open the door. Didn't want the intruder to fall in on him. Or get that close. He'd been driving all night. Needed a shower, not a fist-fight.

And didn't want blood on his father's shiny marble floor. He'd only just laid the man to rest in their Ohio hometown the morning before. Had just lost the last member of his small biological family. Spilling blood would be too much.

Click, turn and...

A woman appeared, stopping with one sandaled foot in the door, one lagging behind. She was young, slender, with soft features and...was that a streak of purple in that hip-length mass of golden-brown curls swirling around her?

"West?"

Dumbfounded—by her presence at all, and by the long-retired use of his shortened name—he stared at her.

"Do I know you?" he managed, frowning instead of showing the back of the door to what he imagined would be a very attention-getting backside.

"I'm Paige Martinson. Your father's memoir collaborator. I was with him when he called you to tell you about me."

He hadn't known that. Was put off by the knowledge with no good reason. "I looked you up online.

Your only social media account is set to private. And there's not much else there." She'd brought her other foot in behind her, but the door still hung open, the early-morning sun bringing a brightness into the room he wasn't ready to face.

He'd just arrived. Needed to...

He didn't know what. Time to figure out what he needed.

"I thought you were older," he said when she didn't explain her lack of internet presence, not even a professional website.

Digging himself a deeper hole. Because he was tired.

And...dammit...grieving. There. No, he wasn't fine, as he'd assured a couple hundred people, over and over, the day before. He'd just lost his father. How could he be fine?

You didn't have to be close to a parent to love them.

"N-not that your age matters a whit," he stumbled on. "Just explains, along with no pictures of you on the internet, why I didn't recognize you."

Now please go. The woman was helping to bring to life Walter's story. She deserved Weston's respect and a good measure of politeness, too.

But he was running low on pretty much anything he'd ordinarily have to give.

Except, apparently, in the libido department. He was wide awake there. His groin, and the parts of his brain that activated it, seemed to be the only part of his body that felt energy.

Because he was out of sorts, out of state, standing in a mansion that had never been home to him, but which was his deceased father's pride and joy. The long black skirt the woman—*Paige*—was wearing… was that Lycra? He didn't remember having ever seen a skirt made of legging material. And the top, a flowing black-and-white tie-dyed tank top with jagged edges instead of a regular hem, and lace, not at all his style.

He was attracted to women in business apparel. Maybe with some hint of cleavage showing. With short or neatly pulled back hair. Top knots. And shoes that covered a woman's toes.

What sort of grown woman colored her toenails with purple and pink stripes?

"Social media doesn't appeal to me. I'm only on there because of my siblings."

This free-spirited-looking woman had siblings? There were more out there like her? For some reason, the idea intrigued his tired mind. He tried to remember what his father had told him about Paige. Other than how much Walter paid her, that he'd insisted on splitting royalties with her when the book went to print the following year, that though she was a ghostwriter by trade, his father had required that she take a byline and share copyright on the book that had already sold to a major New York publisher—all business details—Weston drew a blank.

When she took another step inside, he came to his senses. Took a step forward as well. "It's nice of you to stop by, Ms. Martinson," he told her. "But I've just driven through the night and need to get some rest. I realize we probably have things to discuss regarding the memoir, and I'm happy to schedule an appointment with you later in the weekend, or early next week…"

After he'd had time to settle in.

And figure out how he was going to fit in with his father's legacy. With the mansion.

Her mouth dropped open. And then shut. Not before he noticed those full lips, though. They were as interesting as the rest of her until he reminded himself they were just lips. Lips opened and closed. It was just what they did.

She shook her head. "I fully understand your exhaustion," she told him. "I actually didn't expect you to head down so soon. I'll be as quiet as I can be…"

Taking a step around him, she headed through the foyer, toward the back of the welcoming room. "Excuse me." His tone was no longer welcoming. Or polite.

Spinning, like a figurine of a dancer pirouetting on top of a music box—she took a couple steps toward him before he'd had a chance to make the first move. "Yes?"

"Where do you think you're going?" She might have been welcome to make herself at home when Walter was alive, but the place was Weston's now. And he needed some time alone.

"To feed the dogs."

The dogs? "Come again?"

"Seven is feeding time. Morning and evening. These guys have already suffered enough in their young lives. Walter insisted on routines they could count on to help rebuild their trust..."

"Dogs?" He passed by her, moving toward the back of the house, the entry to the kitchen, wondering how he hadn't known his father had gotten a pet. Two of them apparently, based on the plural *dogs*.

And apparently he owed the ghostwriter a thank-you for looking in on them. Might have been nice, though, if he'd been given a heads-up that there were live beings awaiting his attention.

"I can feed dogs," he told her, looking for them as he rounded the corner and entered a kitchen too enormous for even a large family to need—let alone one man who lived alone.

Walter *had* lived alone, hadn't he?

With a sudden sickening feeling in his gut, he looked back over his shoulder to see the ethereal character following after him. "How long have you had a key to the place?"

"Since I started helping Walter with the dogs. I love them as much as he did, and once he saw that, he didn't want to deny me the pleasure of associating with them."

Right. He nodded, still looking for the animals. Determined to be the one to lead the way through his home.

She'd been heading back toward the kitchen. Which led to the laundry facilities—a room as big as the entire bottom floor of his condo—and still no sign of canine inhabitants.

Walter had hoped to have the house filled with grandkids…

"So you just come to feed them?" he asked then, glad to know they'd been cared for while he, though his dad's only living relative and heir, had been unaware of their existence. "You don't…live here or anything…" She'd used that key with familiarity…

Her hesitation sent more lead to the mound settling in his gut. "Um, *no*," she said slowly, drawing out the word.

Latching on to the word he'd most needed to hear—*no*—Weston dropped the topic, leaving the hesitation in her tone to wither and die.

He was a little concerned that they were standing in the middle of the laundry room with no dogs in sight—and no place else to go except back the way they'd come. He'd only visited the home a couple of times—content to have Walter come home to Ohio for their get-togethers—and had never actu-

ally been in the laundry room, other than to peek
in the door from the kitchen.

Getting to know the house better had been on
his list of to-dos. So he'd know better what to get
rid of in Ohio and what to bring with him. He was
moving in to stay—had known that as soon as he'd
seen the page from his father's will that left him the
place. Made sense, since he was already uprooting
himself and moving to Georgia. The plans had been
in the works for more than a month—ever since
he'd been offered and had accepted a national client
that would allow him to live anywhere. Had been
planning to tell his father the next time they saw
each other. Had wanted to see Walter's face when
he heard the news...

Seemed far too little solace to know that at least
he'd have his father's things around him, but, oddly,
it was helping. Hadn't been that way at all with Mary.
Her things had been constant stabbing reminders of
the lover he'd lost. And his mother? He couldn't remember much about his mother's things, but hadn't
noticed a lot of them around growing up...

"The dogs are through that little archway," Paige
said, motioning toward a little cubby with shelves
bearing extra household supplies. "There's a door
to the outside on the other side of the shelves."

"The dogs are outside?"

So why had she come inside to take care of them?

"Not really," she said, taking a step closer, as

though she was going to pass him and show him the way.

Catapulting into action, Weston rounded the corner, saw the door—frowned as he noticed a lack of any dead bolt or other external security—and pulled. The immediate scrambling of claws and instant whines filled his ears as he stood, taking in the fully enclosed room he knew for certain hadn't been there when he'd last visited the house two years before.

Walter had talked about getting a dog on and off since Rusty had died when Weston had left for college. But…

He counted…

"Seven?" Jumping off from various blankets on couches, one coming to greet him with a wagging tail. Others of varying sizes and colors held themselves back, watching him with big, brown, hesitant gazes.

"He didn't tell you?"

That was pretty obvious, now, wasn't it?

Reaching down to pet the German shepherd—looking mix that was standing right in front of him, he stared at the others, taking in their comfortable surroundings. Homing in on a large doggy door built into the back wall.

"It leads to a quarter-of-an-acre outdoor pen," Paige said, obviously seeing him glance in that direction. Brushing past him, she went to the five dogs who weren't greeting him.

Squatting down, Paige spoke so quietly Weston

couldn't make out her words. She faced each dog individually, taking time to give soft touches and words to the first three. Two of them backed away as she reached out to them, and she lowered herself down on one elbow, talking to first one and then the other, as they both watched her intently.

Overwhelmed, noticing excrement on the floor, he watched as one of the two hold-backers took a step toward Paige and caught himself as he was silently coaxing the dog to let her touch him.

Like he'd know anything at all about the woman's touch. Or had any way to find out?

Seven dogs, ranging in size from ten to seventy pounds, he estimated.

He needed to know names. To figure out what to do with them. How they'd fit into new life plans he'd only just begun to form.

Reaching to the German shepherd mix again, easily the largest of them all, he rubbed the animal's head, looked around for feeding bins. Three large perpetual waterers sat along three of the walls of the room. Dog pads needed to be changed. Floor disinfected. Whoever wasn't house-trained needed to be.

"That's Stover," Paige said, leaning back to look at Weston as she continued to reach a hand out to the wary two. "He's leaving today."

Weston's hand immediately stilled. Pulling it away from the dog, he slid it into his pocket. "Leaving?"

"His family is coming to get him at nine," she said. "I finalized everything yesterday."

What the hell! She was giving away his father's dogs? Sure, Weston had been thinking along those lines, probably, but the choice was his and...

"They're rescues, West." How did a voice hold such compassion with a complete stranger? No one was that familiar. Or that open, either, not when just meeting someone, except maybe his father.

He glanced around the room again, at the various mixed breeds, some too skinny, one with a shaved leg, while Paige continued. "Walter saw a show on TV a couple of years ago. It was a local show about a privately funded nonprofit called Operation Rescue, that is kind of like social services for dogs. They specialize in helping rescues and families find their right matches. He called them and offered to house dogs that couldn't be immediately adopted out for one reason or another. He had this room built soon after. He only takes in seven at a time, but he's the first person Amanda, our contact, calls when any of the local shelters get animals that might be put down. Your dad had a way with them right away. He'd lay on the floor for a couple hours a day if that's what it took to get a dog to trust humans again..."

He'd had no idea. His father had always been one to immerse himself—and by association, West—fully into whatever project he'd taken on to make life better in some way...but living beings?

Had Walter been that lonely?

He should have known. Had a headache. Needed a shower. And some rest.

"So, tell me what I have to do," he said instead. "Are there different diets? Where is the food? And bowls, for that matter. I'll need vet numbers, shelter contacts...has anyone else already been placed?" He ran through the first things that came to mind. And then, before she could supply any answers, asked, "Do they all have names?"

Where was the mop? Where were the puppy pads kept? And who was the untrained one?

One of the friendlier three, a black, brown and white terrier-looking dog, male by the looks of things, sat down and started to scratch as he spoke.

"Have they been checked for fleas?" he added. "And are any on medications?" Made sense, if they'd been mistreated, they might be.

As he continued his barrage, still standing there, shell-shocked, in the doorway, both hands in his pockets, Paige stood up and faced him.

"How about if I take care of everything this morning, while you get yourself settled, showered and rested," she said, her smile just...kind. How long had it been since he'd slowed down enough, tuned in enough, to experience the kindness of others? "I've been helping Walter for the past year and handling them alone this past week. Then later today, when you're feeling better, we can sit down and talk it all through."

Not sure he liked the knowing look in her gaze, or the fact that she was taking control of a situation in his house, he nonetheless jumped right on the respite she'd offered. A smart man knew when he needed to get to his corner and regroup.

But… "There's a puddle over there by the green couch."

"Buddy, yeah," she said. "Every morning in the same place. He's marking his spot. Taking ownership. It's a good thing."

Not if the pup hoped to find a home, Weston thought, looking over the bunch, wondering which one was Buddy. And realizing that she was right. One more feeding wasn't going to change the world, either way.

Nor was kicking her out the front door immediately as critically important. No way he was putting those poor pups further at risk simply because he needed to be alone.

He was tired. Not heartless. Regardless of what his father might or might not have grown to think about him.

"How do I reach you when I'm ready to talk?" Relaxing enough to believe he was actually going to sleep at some point very soon, he gave in long enough to get his wits about him.

"I'll be out here," she said. "I've got my laptop

and have been working here since Walter's death. The dogs and I…we're grieving together." Her voice broke.

And when Weston's heart felt an answering pang, he turned and got the hell out of there.

Paige watched Weston Thomas's very nice backside leave the room, glad to see the broad, military-straight shoulders disappear. Tension slid out of her in a rush, and Buddy, the boy who couldn't quite let himself accept the love he so desperately needed, sat down.

She stared at Buddy. He never relaxed enough to sit unless he was across the room from any human who happened to be sharing it with him. He'd started to come within a couple feet of her in the past week. Had done so with Walter almost from the start. But always on all four feet—able to get himself immediately away in the event a hand that reached toward him turned violent. Never sitting.

And there he was.

Buddy didn't trust people any more than Paige trusted in forever.

He was probably right not to trust Weston Thomas, either. Paige had been dreading the arrival of Walter's uptight son since her employer and friend had suffered the heart attack that had prematurely ended his life. Weston would want to clear out some family mementos, for sure, before

Paige took formal possession of the house that was now hers.

Like she had any use for owned property, period, let alone a mansion and grounds outside of Atlanta, Georgia. She'd tried many times, unsuccessfully, to convince Walter of the fact. He'd always come back with the same question. "How can you know something you've never known?"

How could she know she had no use for property when she'd never owned any? The only way to know what she'd do with it, and what she could gain from it, was to have it and find out.

Their conversations about the matter had always gone the same way. He'd been very definite at the end, too.

He had the right to do whatever the hell he liked with his own property.

The man had definitely liked getting his own way.

And had been the most tenacious person she'd ever met.

She'd been hoping his son would not have inherited those qualities from the father with whom he'd spent little time in the past few years.

Since West's fiancée's death, according to Walter. Prior to that, when West had humored Walter and his various schemes and ideas, he'd still taken time to vacation with him. To go deep-sea fishing. And hiking in various places throughout the world. Both were activities Walter had introduced West to as a child.

And ones, according to Walter, West had given up after Mary died.

Along with the ability to smile, apparently, she thought, with one last glance to the space the man had recently occupied.

He was everything she'd dreaded—and worse. As tenacious and certain he'd get his way as his father had been. Minus Walter's whimsy, his undying optimism and love of life.

"How does a guy who's two years younger than me make me feel like a kid?" She directed the question at Buddy, who didn't move, but the fifteen-pound, skinny blond cocker mix was still sitting within a couple feet of her.

Darcy, an approximately three-year-old beagle mix, came forward and nudged her hand. He'd completely recovered from the surgery on his right front leg, and the hair was even starting to grow back. The leg break had been just one of the atrocities Darcy had lived through. And still, he was willing to give and receive love.

She was right there with him on that one. No matter what life had dealt you, you could still be kind.

Darcy's second nudge was a little less gentle.

She got it. They needed to eat. Not watch her worry about things. All they wanted was to have enough to eat and drink. And to love and be loved. All in one room was fine with them.

They were happy with very little, as long as there was no more cruelty.

And maybe that was why she'd spent the past week with only the dogs. They knew what did and did not matter. And gave unconditional love without limits. People had a lot to learn from the canine population. Walter had known that.

She did, too.

She wasn't so sure she could say the same for Weston Thomas.

Which meant that the sooner they got him out of their orbit, the better.

Chapter Two

Paige wasn't actually getting a lot of work done. West had gone to sleep after his drive, leaving the house in the quiet she'd expected when she'd let herself in that morning. But though there were still three chapters to go before Walter's memoir was complete, and she had all the information she needed to write them, she hadn't listened to any more of the recorded interviews since they'd made them. She wasn't ready yet.

She'd been editing instead. And hadn't been doing a whole lot of that. How could she exist in someone else's head when she was still struggling with the anguish of losing them?

A lesson she hadn't yet learned. How you went deep with the anguish and lived life, too.

She'd learn it. For Walter, she'd get the book done on time. As flexible as Walter had been, he had a thing about meeting deadlines. You always did it. He'd said it defined the type of person you were. A point upon which they'd wholeheartedly agreed.

She just needed a minute—or a week or two of them. And she needed the cloud of Weston Thomas's presence, which had been looming over her and the dogs since Walter's death, to blow over. Once he was gone, and she could figure out why Walter thought owning property would be so important to her own personal journey, she'd be able to submit proposals for her next job. The next chapter in her life.

She could write from anywhere. And while she made a good living, having amassed a positive reputation in the industry, Walter had left enough money in an estate account to keep the bills paid long into the future.

He'd left her none of the rest of his fortune. Just the estate and its account.

She hadn't backed down on that one. If he'd left her other money, she would have donated it immediately. Period. She'd stared him down, and for at least once in his life, *he* had backed down. He'd looked away, muttering, and when she'd seen the page of the will leaving the house to her, she'd noted that he'd left a sizable amount of money to the estate. And not another dime to her.

She'd smiled through her tears.

And was tearing up again, just thinking about the eccentric old man. He'd been in his forties when West was born—his only child. A son who had so been like his wife, Barbara, West's mother, and not a whole lot like Walter. But a son the old man had adored with every fiber of his being.

For Walter she'd be patient with West. Make sure

he had all the time—and whatever possessions—he needed to help him make peace with Walter's death. She'd help him in any way she could. Make him feel welcome.

Because Walter would want that.

And her own life…its next chapter could wait a bit. That's how she rolled. One project to the next. Giving her all to whatever she was working on. After her first unexpected windfall of a project while she was still in college, she had enough in savings, smartly invested, to support a simple lifestyle, and to be able to help her siblings if they ever needed it. Her only real goal was to make enough at each job to add a little bit more to savings. Or, at least, not drain from it.

Maybe, if she lived long enough, she'd be rich.

Maybe not. Didn't much matter to her either way.

She was going to enjoy every single chapter of however long her life's book was going to be.

To find the joy.

Because every moment was precious.

Beyond the moment, she knew not to count on anything.

As she had the thought, the next moment came—in the shape of Weston Thomas. In another pair of dress pants, a lighter gray this time, and ironed looking. His white shirt was also wrinkle free, cuffs rolled halfway up his forearms. The military-cut dark hair might have still been wet from a shower. It was too short to tell.

Those green eyes, though…they were definitely different. The power in that gaze took her breath away. She didn't even know why. Sitting there on the couch with Abe on the other end while Darcy snoozed with her head against Paige's thigh, she pretended to be closing down the document on her laptop. Probably would have been, if she'd had a program open.

She'd just been sitting there, staring, when he'd seemed to barge into the room.

He'd come in quietly enough. It wasn't that the man was a raging bull or anything. He just… exuded…power.

He'd shaved. She'd liked him better with a shadow of stubble.

He didn't look angry. Or even all that tense.

But there was purpose about him.

And she had a feeling she wasn't going to like whatever that purpose was.

Not a problem, really. She knew how to stand her ground. Had been doing so since a carjacker had killed her parents when she was eleven. In spite of the grandma and siblings who'd tried to baby her.

"Where do you want to start?" she asked him as he stopped in the middle of the room, hands on his hips. "Introductions might be a good place." She answered her own question. She owned the place. She was the boss.

But she'd be a kind one. He was Walter's son. And Walter had adored his only child. Had, Paige assumed, left the bulk of his fortune—which included outrageous monthly royalties for Walter's self-filtering water bottle lid invention—to him.

"This is Darcy." She started right in. Because… she owned the place. She had to keep reminding herself. And because she loved the dogs. She'd had a pet as a kid, but after the carjacking, her shattered heart had been in no condition to give any of itself away. "We've been told she's three years old. She was found in a vacated house with multiple injuries. Other than still needing to gain some weight, she's healthy again."

"Why's her leg shaved?"

"She had surgery to repair a severely broken bone." She ran a hand along the dog's head, over her ear and down her torso. Darcy sighed, but didn't open her eyes.

"Down there—" she nodded toward the end of the couch "—is Abe. He came to us with ear mites, intestinal parasites and was suffering from severe malnutrition. He'd had fleas, but they got those under control before they let us have him, lest he inadvertently share them with the others. He's still got some weight to gain, but he's on a strict diet as he can't control his eating. A result of having been starved. He'll eat anything he can get and just keep eating until he vomits, and then go right on eating.

"Buddy's the little blond cocker mix over there." She nodded to the little guy curled up in a dog bed in the corner. "We have no idea what happened to him, but he's more afraid of humans than any animal I've ever met. He's coming around, though." She'd thought she might actually get to pet him off leash during morning feed. "He follows sit and stay commands long enough to be leashed, but if you reach out to love on him, he backs up. You could go after him, of course. He won't run away. He'll just back himself into a corner and press against the wall and shake. I work with him every day, though, and we're getting closer."

West looked from dog to dog as she spoke. His gaze was not moving from them as she gave their history. She liked him a little better for that.

"Annie over there is some kind of poodle/bichon mix. She's our smallest dog, at just over ten pounds. She's also the one I worry about most, weight-wise. She's afraid to eat. She'll drink like there's no tomorrow, but feeding time is always a touch-and-go situation with her. I've learned that if I change the kind of food I give her every mealtime, she'll take a few bites before she backs up."

"Maybe she just doesn't like dog food."

"Believe it or not, Annie won't even take chicken and rice for more than a few bites. If I take her out into the house, lock her away from the others, she'll usually do better, maybe consume half a serving, but it takes an hour or more."

"Have you tried nutrients in water for her? Since she'll drink?"

Impressed by his intuitiveness where the dogs' needs were concerned, seeing a hint of Walter in him, she said, "Every day. Twice a day. That's why she's as healthy as she is. We think she was either hit regularly or maybe attacked by another animal during feeding times when she was little."

"And that guy over there—" she pointed to a forty-pound Australian shepherd "—is Checkers. He's eleven, deaf and partially blind, which makes him an unlikely adoption candidate. He was well loved and is loving, when he's awake. His owner died and Walter took him in to make certain that he didn't get put down.

"And the pug cuddled up to him is Erin. She'd been both abused and neglected. She was rescued when her owner went to jail for possession. I'm not sure what all happened to her, but if you look closely you can see little scars over her body. She's surprisingly friendly, though. And smart. She'll probably be our next adoptee."

Hands in his pockets now, he glanced around, while she studied him, wondering about a person who didn't need to be touching fur with so many loving beings in the room.

"Where's Stover?" The German shepherd. He'd pet Stover that morning.

"With his new family. He left an hour ago."

Which was really why Paige had been sitting there crying. Or why she'd started, anyway. She was happy for Stover. Just a little unhappy for herself. It would pass. She knew that well. She'd sit with the sadness and it would settle into a place where the memories of those she'd loved and lost hung out.

He looked around him again, nodded and said, "Well, if you want to give me the rundown on who eats how much of what and when, show me where everything is and, if you could, help me make a list of everything you just told me, I'll take over and you can be on your way."

She felt a frown take over her face of its own accord. And once there, she couldn't seem to change it into a smile. She told herself to give him some slack. He'd just buried his father the day before. Was away from home. Had traveled all night.

Compassion rose within her at all of the above, but not enough to get over his rudeness.

"I don't need, want or intend to allow you to take over." She didn't raise her voice. Was careful to monitor her tone in light of the skittish spirits in the room. But she wasn't smiling. Not even a little bit.

When his eyebrows rose, and his mouth dropped open, Paige stood—gently enough to help Darcy settle down to snooze on her own, and then, back straight, left the room.

He'd follow her. He had nowhere else to go, unless he wanted to cage himself up in the outdoor dog pen.

At the moment she didn't care if he chose to do just that—except that would trap her friends with him.

And they were her first priority.

She wasn't about to let the conversation she and Weston Thomas were about to have happen within earshot of innocents, human or canine, who'd had enough tension in their lives.

They deserved better than that.

And she was finding out what it meant to own a home—she couldn't just walk away.

West watched the woman go, tempted to go after her and get slapped for trying to kiss her. She was maddening. And captivating. Even when he was showered and rested.

He barely knew her. And he wanted her.

The feelings she raised in him were part of why he remained where he was. Not only were they wholly inappropriate, but he'd also had his share of intensity—growing up with his father's constant hype and hope and confidence that was inevitably followed by defeat—and with the unexpected loss of Mary, too. Walter still hadn't made it big, hadn't had a success when West had given his fiancée his whole heart—the first time he'd ever done so with anyone. A historical librarian, she'd been right up his alley. Her nurturing had been the first feminine influence he'd ever felt strongly in his life and he'd been a sucker for it. Growing up with only loving memories for a mother, told from his father's point of view, apparently did that to a guy.

Standing there, the center of attention for at least three sets of eyes, he alternated between bothered and bemused. He admired Paige's fire but found her words so over-the-top ludicrous they were almost amusing.

As if she had any say whatsoever in what he did or did not do with his house and his dogs. He might not have known the canines existed, but that didn't make them any less his responsibility. Or his right to disperse with.

Or keep. If he chose.

After he called the shelter and found out exactly how much ownership he had of the dogs. And how the whole adoption thing worked.

Checkers, the old Australian shepherd, was awake, cocking his head as he looked at West, and West answered the question he felt coming at him from that old guy by heading over, kneeling down and petting him; Checkers licked at his wrist with a thick tongue.

"We'll figure it all out, won't we, boy?" he asked, in spite of the dog's deafness. Checkers would see West's lips move. Maybe. Those solemn eyes looking up at him certainly seemed to be taking West in, regardless of partial blindness.

Obviously, he'd be keeping Checkers. His dad had made a commitment to the old dog, and for Walter, and maybe himself, too, West wanted to honor that commitment. He had fond memories of Rusty, after all.

Living in a condo, a dog hadn't seemed like a fair option. But, as a part of West's new beginning, he wasn't opposed to the idea of dog ownership.

In honor of his father. Some of the joy he'd been picturing on his dad's face when he eventually broke the news about moving to Atlanta was back. West also imagined Walter with him while he went around to each dog, getting as close as he could to the ones who didn't trust him enough to be welcoming, talking to them as though they could understand his words. Introducing himself as Walter's son.

And when he was through, he knew he couldn't put off facing the woman who'd walked out on him. If she'd left, he'd have to grovel and call her back. Just long enough to get the dogs' information from her.

It didn't even occur to him that she might refuse to come back. She'd do it for the animals, not for him.

He didn't have to call her. Or even go looking. She was standing in the kitchen, leaning back against one of the professional restaurant kitchen-sized counters, drinking from a purple ceramic mug that was as big as her hand.

"Oh, good, there's coffee?" he asked. Walter had thrived on the stuff, but West hadn't known what supplies would be in the house. And since he'd hired movers to pack his condo for him, and was expecting them to arrive by Sunday, he hadn't brought anything with him but essentials, keepsakes and clothes.

"I'm drinking tea," she said. "Chamomile. It's good for calming tension. I'll make you a cup if you'd like."

He wasn't a tea drinker unless he was sick. And then he just wanted regular tea. Strong and black. The way he liked his coffee.

"I'd prefer coffee. My father had the stuff running through his veins, so I'm hoping there's some here."

Unless she'd cleaned him out already. Emptied the kitchen. Donated it all to a shelter. Taking ownership of the leftover groceries like she seemed to think she could do with the dogs and, in fact, the whole house.

Which was fine. He'd already decided he'd make a grocery run and get the coffee and little bit he needed until his stuff arrived. He generally ordered out for meals. Much more efficient when you were eating for one. And at home, that was just how he wanted it. One.

She pointed to a cupboard. And to the state-of-the-art coffee maker in an alcove holding a mug tree with one missing.

The purple one, he guessed.

He opened the cupboard she'd indicated. Found his favorite brand and blend—and Walter's, too—as both loose grounds and in individualized coffee maker cups, and chose the grounds and a disposable filter from the pile. He had a strong hunch he was going to need a whole pot's worth of refills ready and waiting.

And he'd had a moment to think, too.

"Look, I didn't mean to be so harsh back there, as though I'm trying to just cut you off from the dogs. It's clear you care about them. If you want to stop by to see them…you're welcome to visit anytime you'd like."

The look of compassion that filled that compelling dark blue gaze startled him.

Was she feeling sorry for him?

Yeah, he'd just lost his last living relative, but that didn't mean he wouldn't be fine. He would be. He'd get along. Life was what you made it and he had a good one. Currently with a drastic change, yes. But some of it was good change. Great change. New challenges. New sights and sounds and tastes…

"I think you're laboring under a huge misapprehension, West," she said softly. Her use of that name…it stung. In a weirdly gentle way.

"My name's Weston."

He'd startled her. By the way she stepped back, shuttering her gaze, he figured he'd probably offended her, too. He could almost see his father's frown at his brusqueness. And he didn't apologize. He was fighting for something greater than politeness. And as soon as he figured out what it was, he'd find a way to be polite about it.

"I know your full name, of course," she said, her tone a little more distant as she held her cup of tea with both hands and sipped. To ease tension.

As if a cup of tea really had the power to do that.

"I know your birth weight, and the first words you said, too. It's all in the chapter where Walter had a son. But he always called you West. Even when he was just referring to having spoken to you, nothing to do with the memoir. I just assumed…" Her shrug nudged his guilt into full gear.

Was this woman for real?

And why wouldn't she be?

He was the one taking an attitude. Being in his father's home…feeling robbed of the chance to tell Walter that he was moving to Georgia…of the chance to see his dad more often…

None of that was her fault. Or had anything to do with her.

"Aside from what to call you, we still have an issue here," she continued, no warmth immediately discernible in her voice. "I'd suggest you call your father's lawyer. His name is Grant Lieberman. I have an appointment with him first thing Monday morning, but I'm sure, given the circumstances, he'll see you immediately. I've got his number..."

He didn't need to call Grant. He knew what was in the will. His father had sent the assets page a while back, soon after it was drawn up, leaving him the house, with an expense budget that pretty much took up the bulk of Walter's fortune.

Still, it was curious... "I have his number. And a Monday-morning appointment. At eight."

Eyes widening, she froze with her cup halfway to those distracting lips. "Mine's at eight, too."

Everything stilled. The air. His breath. Her energy. His heart rate. As though frozen in time, they stood there, staring at each other.

Assessing each other.

And, at least in Weston's case, assessing Walter.

What had his father done now?

"He left me the house, Weston."

Her words didn't fully compute. Not yet. They wouldn't until he could figure out what Walter's thought process had been. Because he knew that the house was his; he just didn't know why she thought it was hers. She'd have good reason, though. Something to do with his father.

Even in death, in probate, Walter was being inventive.

And if history repeated itself, chances were ninety-nine to one that he'd fail.

And Walter's odd, compassionate, wholly distracting memoir collaborator, the ghostwriter, was going to get hurt.

Or Weston was.

His gut sank.

Chapter Three

Paige was the first one to move. She sipped her tea, not caring that what turned out to be an unintentional gulp burned her tongue.

"Why would we both have appointments at the same time?" She asked the question aloud, figuring they were both wondering.

"It's not uncommon with a reading of a will." Weston sounded calm. Almost unconcerned. His posture was a bit stiff. "All beneficiaries are called to be present." The last statement came out around a quick sip from his cup.

Her stomach calmed some. "That makes sense, though you'd think Mr. Lieberman might have said something when he called to set up the appointment. Kind of awkward during the grieving process to be walking into an appointment with someone you've just met." His stance didn't change, and she hastened to assure him, "Your dad left me this house, including the dogs, of course, and a stipend for the property upkeep, but that's it. I refused to continue with the memoir until I saw that he didn't leave the bulk of his fortune, or the invention royalties, to me.

I'm sure that's all yours. And the house... I guess he figured you didn't have a purpose for it, living in Ohio and all..."

How did a man stand so still, so expressionless, for so long?

And how did his silent grief, hidden behind stoicism, still call out to her?

What gave this man the ability to pull her heartstrings so profoundly? She didn't even like him. Except that he was Walter's son.

They had nothing in common, Weston and her. All the months she'd spent hearing about him from Walter, all the mementoes she'd seen, the letters she'd read...report cards, even. He'd excelled at institutionalized learning. She'd been bored by it. She'd done it. Had a creative arts bachelor's degree from a prestigious school, but that had simply been a means to an end.

Weston appeared to be a black-and-white kind of guy.

She floated through life in shades of purple and pink. With a bit of blue mixed in. Like with Walter's death. Definitely blue.

She jumped when West finally moved. Weston. Weston moved. He left, actually. Just walked out of the room with his cup of coffee sitting on the counter. Couldn't blame him, she supposed. She'd done the same to him just a few minutes before, abruptly leaving the kennel without a word.

He'd apparently thought the house was his. Had to be a mental, if not emotional, blow to find out that it wasn't. He'd need time to process.

She could give him that. She had nowhere to be, except at the keyboard. Walter's memoir wasn't going to write itself and deadlines didn't wait. She'd put in written notice at her apartment. Had to be out by the weekend, but she could take the back bedroom, the only bedroom on the ground floor— probably originally intended for live-in staff—for the time being. And hang out with the dogs. The kennel had always been her favorite place in the house.

And her stuff…she traveled light, rented furnished apartments. She could unload the majority of her things in one of the garages for now. They were boxed up tight and would be all right. The clothes and toiletries—those she'd already brought in while he'd been sleeping. Had left them in the back hall, not wanting to take them upstairs and risk waking him. The hanging things were all in the back bedroom closet already.

So, yeah, things were going to be fine. It would all work out, she reassured herself. She always made sure it did.

"Here's a copy of what you'll be seeing on Monday." West's words hit her at the same time his presence did. Like a ton of bricks. A wall she couldn't penetrate.

So why wasn't she pushing back as hard as she could? Why was she reaching for the paper he held? Giving him the benefit of the doubt?

She glanced at him before she looked at the sheet he held.

She was giving him space because he was Walter's son. And her weird sense of comfort, being close to him; that was also because of Walter.

Suddenly finding him more attractive than any man she could remember…standing there closer to him than she'd been to date, close enough to smell his pine-scented soap, or whatever, feeling his body warmth… Well, that must just be her way of fighting herself out of the cavern of grief.

You found something good to feel, even if you had to make it up.

"Read," he said, his tone kinder sounding all of a sudden. Or maybe she was making that up, too.

Glancing down, she recognized the formatting, the font, the header—all things she, as a writer, would note—and then, as she read the first paragraph, frowned.

She knew the words. Had a copy of them in her bag out in the kennel with her computer. Except that where her name should be, it read "Weston Lake Thomas." "Lake" for his mother's maiden name, she knew.

"But…" Frowning, she glanced up at him. Read again, noted the date.

Her copy of the asset page of Walter's will had the exact same date. She was sure of it. There was a time stamp on his, 2:04 p.m. Did hers have one?

Until that moment she hadn't realized how much she'd been counting on understanding any final life lessons Walter wanted her to learn from property ownership. He'd seemed so certain that it would change her life in some marvelous way.

And, dammit, she'd believed him.

Handing West the piece of paper, she started to tremble. Had to get to her computer bag and the file of most important papers she'd stashed there after leaving her apartment key at the office.

Without another word, or even a backward glance, she set down her tea and left the room.

She'd done it again. Just walked out on him. Like he was supposed to know what to do with that. Other than dwell on how much she infuriated him. The situation was difficult enough without her flighty attitude.

Yeah, he'd walked out without a word, too. But only to get the proof he'd needed. He'd come right back.

She didn't return immediately. He drank his coffee. Poured a second cup, mostly to be doing something besides waiting around for her in the event she reappeared, and started in on that, too.

Until it dawned on him that she'd read that the

house—and the dogs—weren't hers, and then made a beeline…straight to the pets. Was she removing them from the residence? Had she already done so?

He had no idea what kind of vehicle she drove. A beater, he'd guess, something older. But it could be big enough to transport six dogs.

Setting his half-empty cup down next to hers, he strode out to the kennel…

And stopped abruptly in the doorway. On the floor, with the little pug on her lap, the big beagle's head on her thigh, the skinny little black terrier sitting next to her, with Checkers close by and the others standing a few feet away, from her and each other, Paige sat with tears on her face.

He must have made some sound that alerted her to his presence as she quickly wiped her cheeks. And her hands on the dogs moved more fully over them, as though she was gathering them all into her as quickly as she could. Ready to wrap her arms around them and protect them from the big, bad bully.

That would be him. The big, bad bully.

He wasn't one. He knew that.

She should, too, after having spent the past year or more hearing about him.

Surely his father wouldn't have built him up to be someone anyone would fear. He was the most quiet, private man he knew. He lived by the book, delivered on his word, surprised no one, except maybe with a good financial outcome they hadn't expected. He smiled at people. Helped where he could.

And otherwise kept to himself.

He didn't hurt anyone.

Other than Walter, he feared. He hoped not. But…had he? Inadvertently?

He'd thought his father understood him. Was proud of him. They were vastly different people. But had always respected each other.

Loved each other.

So why hadn't he known his father was running a kennel?

Had Walter been that lonely for family? Dying lonely because his only son had been too wrapped up in his own life to see that his old man needed him?

His father had always been welcome in Ohio. Weston had told him, multiple times, that if Walter wanted to move home, they could get a place together…

And Walter had always seemed so happy in Georgia, so busy, constantly meeting new people, bringing them into his life.

"You have something to say or are you just going to stand there watching us?" Paige's truculent words almost made Weston smile.

Which was as absurd as everything else that had already transpired that day.

"I'm not sure what to say," he answered honestly. "I've already told you that I'm not going to deprive you or the dogs of each other." His need to offer her comfort took precedence over everything else. Another anomaly for him.

He was the guy who always looked at the practical side of things. His world was lined with facts, not emotion.

"I honestly have no idea who's going to deprive who of what," she said. Her despondency didn't seem to be lessening any. He wanted to go to her.

To pet Checkers. Let the old guy know that he still had family.

But he didn't feel welcome in their midst. And didn't want to intrude. Not until he had to. Details could wait until Monday.

"If you want to carry on…tend to them on your own, as you normally would…until Monday, that's fine by me." He'd been too harsh before. He'd known it at the time. "We can sort everything out after we meet with Grant." Maybe, if she wanted, she could still be mostly in charge of the kennel.

Though, having her coming and going…he wasn't sure how wise that would be. Definitely not a black-and-white thing.

Or a choice based on fact. Because the fact was, he could take care of the animals himself. Or hire someone to help if need be.

If he kept the kennel, that was. Nothing so far said he had to do that.

Walter seemed to nudge him from the grave at

that thought. Weston tabled the topic just as Paige stood, came toward him.

She handed him a piece of paper that looked eerily familiar. Taking it, glad that she backed away as quickly as she'd approached, giving him space from the distractions that she bred, he made a quick once-over.

Then read more slowly.

And for a third time, read again.

Checked the date and time stamp.

And pulled out his phone to give his father's so-called attorney a call. Didn't matter a whit to him that it was late Saturday afternoon. Some things weren't going to wait until Monday.

With Erin cuddled against her body with one arm and Annie on the other side of her, at her feet, Paige paced while West was on the phone with Grant. Darcy and Abe followed her. Buddy looked on. She focused on them, promising silently that she wasn't going to abandon them. No matter what it took. Not only were they blessed symbols of unconditional love, but they were also vulnerable. And on their second chances.

She tried to figure out how the conversation was going, but after his initial accounting of his complaint—she couldn't have given it any better from her own point of view—he'd done little more than give an occasional "uh-huh" or "I see," with an "I understand" thrown in once or twice.

She liked his voice. Deep. Calming. It instilled confidence.

Five minutes into the mostly non-conversation, she realized that West had his father's voice. Maybe that was why she was finding it easier to trust him than she did most people she'd just met.

Well, that and the fact that she knew he'd insisted on snuggles and reading every night before he'd go to bed until he was four. At which time he'd suddenly announced that he was too old to cuddle like a baby. Walter had wanted to point out that *he* was a grown man and still needed hugs, but he'd let West lead his own way. One that had turned out to be vastly different from Walter's.

And hers, for that matter. She and Walter were a lot alike.

Which was why she knew that there was no way the inventor would have lied to her about the house and dogs. Walter had never been mean or harsh, but he'd gotten downright firm with her when he'd challenged her about not wanting to own anything she couldn't pick up and take with her.

By the time West hung up she was beyond trying to decipher what their lives were going to look like and had moved into her happy place, focusing on how firm and perfectly shaped his butt was—not an easy feat in dress pants.

He faced her from the doorway, his phone still in hand. "Have you ever met Grant Lieberman?"

"No. I'd never even heard of him until I got his call last week."

Had Walter been taken in by a scammer pretending to be a lawyer?

And where would that leave the dogs? And the estate?

"He's part of an elite firm of experts, housed out of Phoenix, Arizona, but working all over the country. Sierra's Web. You ever hear of them?"

She shook her head a second time, the movement only slightly mimicking the major trembling going on inside her at these words.

She supposed some elite expert was better than a scammer. She just didn't know why Walter had needed one to draw up something as simple as a will with only two beneficiaries.

"Apparently my father chose to give us each separate but equal pages of the same document," he continued, seeming as lost as she felt. As confused. "At Walter's behest, Lieberman can only reveal the will to us in its entirety when we are together, in person, with him."

Excitement blew through her. Her page was legal? Legitimate? She really belonged there? And it dissipated almost as quickly. It couldn't be right. Not with West having the same inheritance.

"What's the catch?"

He shook his head. "I have no idea."

"You were on the phone for a long time to know nothing."

He shrugged, looked at her, and a grin tilted the corners of his lips. Not a lot. Not in humor. But in…comradery?

The expression zoomed straight to the part of her that had been connecting to him since she'd first unlocked the front door that morning. For months she'd thought about meeting West Thomas. Walter's son.

For many reasons. Number one being that Walter was so completely enamored of his son. She hadn't seen a parent's love in action like that in more than twenty years. Had thought she'd imagined some of the adoration she told herself she'd felt from her family. Embellished it over the years with youthful perspective.

Being part of the nitty gritty of Walter's life, as much as anyone could ever be without actually being family, she'd wanted to see what West and Walter really shared. Seeing from the inside, rather than from the outside looking in.

She was the first to break eye contact. As soon as she realized they'd been staring at each other. Holding on. To nothing. To not knowing.

She missed him as she turned around, made it to the couch. Sat down.

And told herself to stay strong when West joined her.

There'd be no further emotional connections with this man. Ever.

Chapter Four

Weston didn't feel right, sitting on a dog couch in a kennel room with a woman who was so unlike him that they didn't even breathe in the same atmospheres. He didn't feel like himself.

And yet, for the moment, he couldn't think of anyplace else to go. His entire world had suddenly morphed into an incoherent realm and Paige seemed to hold the key to it. She'd spent a hell of a lot more time with his father than he had over the past year.

If you were going to add up hours, she'd have spent more time with Walter in one year than he had in the last three or four years combined. Maybe more. *Probably* more.

So, there he sat. Uncomfortable. Needing facts that weren't presenting themselves. How did he build his new structure without the necessary building materials?

Being with the dogs his father had temporarily adopted—and Checkers, who was permanent—was about the only thing that made sense to him.

"Lieberman explained that he'd never seen anything like my father's will. Dad asked for two experts, Lieberman and his colleague, Diane Gale, and both of them researched extensively to make certain that his will is airtight. Dad paid for Lieberman's time, a set number of hours a week, for the next two months as well, and Diane's fees are paid until the end of this week. Once the will is read on Monday, Grant is being paid to assist you in any way you might want. And Diane will be there through the week for my benefit. If I find I need her services after that, I'll need to pay for them myself."

And that was just the tip of the mountain from which he was falling.

"Your father's already bought me a lawyer's hours for the next two months?"

"Yes."

But not him. He had to pay his own way.

Which was fair, he supposed. More than fair. Considering that she'd had so much time with Walter.

"Why would I need a lawyer for months? Is there something wrong with the estate?"

"I have no idea."

"But the estate is mine?"

"Grant refused to explain the details that go along with the two pages we've now both seen. He claimed attorney-client privilege. In order for the will to be valid as written, it has to be read to both of us, in person, at the same time."

He'd already said that. His brain just couldn't make sense of it. What had his dad intended?

"You don't think he expects us to get married or anything like that, do you? Could that be grounds for validating the will?"

So they'd had the same thought. At least they had that in common.

"It occurred to me that that might be what we're facing."

"That's ludicrous." Wow. Second time they'd agreed. Maybe they could set a new record.

"So maybe the reason we need lawyers is to fight the will."

He hated to say his next thought, but knew it had to be considered, expected the lawyer to suggest such a thing in event of a marriage requirement being attached to the will. "What we're probably going to have to do is think about having him declared incompetent so we can set the will aside." The words stuck in his throat as he said them. His father was odd. Walked to the beat of his own drum. He was not incompetent.

And if the will was invalidated, then he, as the only living heir, would get everything. In normal circumstances, anyway. He wouldn't put it past Walter to have a contingency will.

Would his dad really do that? Draw up a second will in case of contingency?

No, that was him thinking, not Walter. He was the contingency guy.

And if his father wanted his ghostwriter to have some of his wealth, West would see that she got it. In some fashion.

"Walter wasn't incompetent."

"No, but sometimes he appears that way. It's not typically all there to think you can force two people who have never met to marry. If that's what he wanted."

He heard his words and cringed. *Marriage* wasn't a word that fit in his life. He'd eschewed it years ago. Permanently.

"So maybe it's not about marriage."

"Can you think of any coherent reason for a man to give two people separate pages of a will, making them both think they were inheriting an estate someday, while hiring two nationally renowned legal experts to draw up an airtight document, paying for their future services and then commanding that both of the beneficiaries be physically present for the reading of the will?"

"Not offhand, *nooo*." She drew out the word.

"I'm not getting married." And he wasn't giving up the house, either.

"Really. That's good to know." She could have been talking about soup.

"I mean it."

"You're what, thirty-one? That's a little young to

know that you won't ever meet someone who turns your crank in a different direction."

Turns of his crank were absolutely none of her business.

But he got a little stiff down there, thinking about her touching it. And brushed aside the highly inappropriate thought, too.

"I'm not getting married to keep this house."

"Neither am I."

"I'm not giving up the property, either." The statement was a promise. One with nothing solid behind it until he knew what he was up against. But she needed to know he wasn't walking away.

"Neither am I."

Stalemate.

Unacceptable.

The woman was infuriating. And he wasn't hating sitting there with her. It was better than getting lost in the mansion that had felt like home to his dad.

"How old are you?" She knew his age. And was going to the reading of his father's will, with a prepaid lawyer. He figured those two facts justified the question.

She didn't answer right away. He thought about her knowing his birth weight. Was just about ready to shoot that out there when she said, "Thirty-three."

Before he could come up with something else brilliant to say, she added, "And for the record, I also have no intention, whatsoever, of getting married."

The statement further provoked him, for no good reason. He knew why he was remaining single—the woman he'd planned to spend his life with was gone—but had no idea why she was so off the tradition of partnering up with another.

"You have a bad relationship?" It was the obvious answer.

"Nope."

"Maybe you just haven't met the right person." Someone who turned her crank in another direction.

He had no idea why he was pushing the issue. He knew other people who were happily single; no reason she couldn't be one of them.

"I met him. I just don't believe in making promises you can't keep."

Everything about the statement annoyed him. So much so that he didn't know what to deal with first. "You have so little faith in people that you don't think anyone can keep a promise?" he asked.

"I know for a fact that no one can promise forever. Because it doesn't exist in the human realm. And I find that the older I get, the more certain I am that I can't settle for less than that. I need forever. And the only forever I can count on is my own because I'm the only one who will go with me when I die."

He had no words. Or even any thoughts in response. Instead, he sat there with an overwhelming sense of sadness.

And a need to prove her wrong.

Right and wrong, they weren't words he used a lot. His life was run by facts more than judgment. He'd believed in his father so many times as a kid, had bragged to his peers about this or that invention, sure it was the one, only to be hugely embarrassed, more and more as time, and failed inventions, went on...

And he couldn't disprove what she said. Not any part of it.

"But...you love." The fact wasn't pertinent. It was all he had.

"Of course, I do."

He nodded. Partially appeased. And realized that he hadn't had a thought about the loss of his father for a whole five minutes. More time than he'd managed since he'd gotten the call from authorities letting him know that Walter had passed.

"He had a bad heart. You knew that, right?"

Her question came from left field. No way she could have known that he'd been thinking about Walter's death at that exact moment.

"Clearly, since he had a massive heart attack."

"No, I mean, he knew his time was imminent. He'd been having problems. Had been seeing a specialist. He told me he'd called you, that he'd told you."

Weston stared at her, his skin cold. He buried a hand in Checkers's fur, moved it up and down, massaging. His throat was too tight, too dry, to speak the words he might have said.

"You didn't know."

Lips pursed, he shook his head.

Walter had been dying and Weston hadn't known.

His truth, his agony, lay there out in the open where she could see it and he was shrinking from it. Freezing with exposure.

"You thought I knew. And that I didn't bother coming to see him."

Her shrug said a lot about her. She wasn't judging. Or maybe was just trying not to.

"I've already given up the lease on my office space in Ohio, have referred most of my clients to others and have sold the condo. I'm going to be working with a national client that will take all of my time, and I will, very shortly, be hiring a staff to work for me. Here in Atlanta. The long-term plan is to seek out other national clients as I grow the business. With one lucrative company vouching for me, other doors will be opened. I was waiting to tell Dad when I saw him for his birthday next week."

He needed her to understand why he couldn't let her take his father's house from him. Why he'd fight whatever they were facing, using every dime he had if it came to that.

The property, the house, the dogs he hadn't

known about—they were the only family he had left. And he could see himself living out a decent life right there, taking in dogs and running his company. A life that would suit him even when he was old and gray. He was actually starting to see his future.

The life he was meant to live.

And marriage wasn't a part of it.

She'd given no audible response to his maudlin tale, and he wasn't looking in her direction to discern a response. He couldn't let the woman nudge him off course.

He also couldn't just ignore her existence. Or the fact that she'd been led to believe that the house and dogs were hers.

"No matter what is revealed on Monday, I want you to know that I'm not out to hurt you."

"I never thought you were."

Someone whined. He had no idea who, but it came from her side of the couch. "They probably need to eat, huh?"

"Yeah."

"I'd like to help, or at least observe the process."

"You can help. Walter and I usually did it together."

"And tomorrow," he quickly jumped in. "If you'd like to come back and feed, or spend time in here, feel free. You've got your key."

They'd deal with that on Monday, too. Her having a key. And her time with the dogs.

With the two littlest dogs in her arms, one on each side, she stood. Headed toward a cupboard on the back wall. "I'm staying here, Weston," she told him.

Told him. Didn't ask.

"Excuse me?"

She'd lined up bowls on the countertop and was reaching for plastic bins that looked like dog food containers. "I have as much legal right to be here as you do at the moment," she pointed out, not unkindly.

He joined her at the counter. First priority at the moment was learning how to care for the dogs. He saw that each bowl had a name. And that taped to the inside cupboard door was a list of who got how much of what and when.

She could have mentioned that to him earlier.

The fact that she hadn't, told him that he wasn't the only one being proprietary. He made a big mental note to not let down his guard.

"I wasn't talking about legal rights," he countered as she handed him one of the larger food bins and a measuring cup.

"That's for Buddy, Abe and Darcy," she told him, leaving him to gather the right bowls and follow measuring instructions. "And I am talking about legal rights," she said then. "Partially because I've already given up my apartment and, today, unloaded my SUV with all of my stuff out in the garage and in the back bedroom off the kitchen."

Three bowls loaded and in hand, he almost dropped them as he stared at her. "You've already moved in?"

The five dogs swarming at their feet, whining, sniffing, generally tripping over themselves, were nowhere near enough distraction from the bullet she'd just shot straight through him. She was living in his house?

Possession was nine tenths of the law and he'd had it. Or so he'd thought.

Had planned to spend Sunday alone with his father's home. Learning things.

"Today," she confirmed.

And he suddenly knew what that long drawn-out "no" in response to his question that morning about her living at the mansion had been about.

Perhaps it would have been wiser not to have ignored the opening that strange "no" had given him. Asked her what she meant by it, why she'd said it like that. He'd chosen to ignore whatever it might have been. He wouldn't do that again.

Another note to self.

He had the feeling that he was going to need a list for all those mental notes he was compiling. Rules by which he'd keep himself sane and prevent as much damage as possible in the days to come.

To manage his way through more Walter tumult. He'd known, the second he'd seen Paige with the dogs—maybe before that, even—that she wasn't a user. Walter might have attracted a gold digger or two along the way—people who'd thought his cheerfulness made him manipulatable—but he'd also rid himself of them.

He missed his dad as he bent to put bowls down along the side wall, several feet apart, as she designated.

And said, "So, we'll be living under the same roof for the remainder of the weekend," as he rejoined her at the counter, wanting her to know that he wasn't going to kick her out. Only Annie and Checkers were left to be fed. He grabbed the old dog's bowl. Paige gave him a food container. He noted which one. And checked the list for the feeding amount.

"It'll be longer than just the weekend," she told him. "Regardless of what stipulations the will puts on us, I have no place else to go."

"Neither do I."

She nodded.

He didn't.

No way was he going to be living indefinitely with the intoxicatingly bothersome woman in his midst.

Chapter Five

Paige thought about leaving. Heading out was her strong point. Something she could count on. She never had a problem saying goodbye to a current circumstance and moving on to the next. It was a key aspect of herself that drove her life.

It was one of the traits she most admired about herself. In spite of the horrible tragedy she'd suffered, she'd still perfected an ability to be happy and productive, self-sufficient, without forming lasting attachments, which brought her ultimate peace.

West had excused himself after the dogs ate and she'd been mostly glad to see him go. She'd have liked a bit more conversation to discuss different will scenarios and options that might allow them both to come out satisfied.

But had no idea how to initiate such a conversation. She diffused some lavender oil into the air, but turned off the pot when Buddy started to sneeze. Put on soft instrumentals, instead. Read some Deepak Chopra, with a hand on Darcy's head and Erin and Annie curled on her skirt—one on her thighs and the other at her calves. She'd been relying on the author for years to help her live stress-free and had been waiting for his new book on meditation for months. She cleared her chakras.

And every few minutes had her transcendentalism invaded by thoughts of Weston Thomas. Because he was putting her immediate safety and security in peril, she determined. The man's presence was threatening to trap her down on level two of Maslow's hierarchy of needs—making her worry about her living space being secure—which then prevented her ascent to the top of Maslow's pyramid and her own self-actualization.

She didn't go to bed without getting there, if she could help it. And almost always, she could help it.

Not so much that night. Reading wasn't working. Her mind was wandering too much.

But she couldn't give in. She'd spent too many years studying, facing her deepest truths, on a quest for peace, and now that she'd learned how to find it, to get to that inner place where everything was okay, no way was she going to let a will, or a handsome stranger, suddenly disrupt her hard won happiness. She, like all humans, according to Maslow, needed to love and be loved. The dogs fulfilled that need. She had to feel good about herself. Done. So what was missing?

She had to find that, to be able to float up to reach a good night's rest. Paige retrieved her yoga mat and laid it out in the middle of the dogs' room.

They were part of her emotional health tool kit, and she liked to think she was part of theirs, too.

She started her breathing before she'd even finished changing into purple yoga pants and a pink top—and was already much calmer as she lowered herself to the mat. Erin wanted to join in, so Paige scooted over to make room and, the music low, closed her eyes, breathed in deeply and slowly lay back.

The second her body was supine, her breasts facing upward, she felt…exposed.

And kind of sexy.

Her nipples tightened.

Ignoring them, she took breaths. Blew them out. Listened to the music. Pulled her knees up, grasped her feet and spread her legs for the *happy baby* pose that always helped her ease tension in her back.

And immediately thought of West standing in that room, almost on the spot where she was lying, just hours before. His masculinity, while readily apparent when he was there, took over a space in such a quiet way she hadn't recognized it sneaking up on her at first.

What if the will *did* say they had to marry to keep the house?

Signing a legal document joining their names together wouldn't be the end of the world. She'd know it wouldn't be a real union. There'd be no promises made of faithfulness or being together until death.

Walter hadn't mentioned West's part in the plan, though, which made her uneasy.

And disappointed. The older man had been so adamant that she give herself a chance to own property. To have ground that she owned. He'd been so certain that her life would expand in ways she couldn't imagine.

He'd hooked her in with the possibility of being able to fly higher during her time on earth.

And look at her...already she was fighting for her right to keep the house.

Because Walter was right?

She'd given the wise and inventive old man her word she'd stick it out for a year. Mostly to comfort him, because he'd been so agitated at the thought that he could see something missing in her life that she could not see. And somewhat because he was a smart man, with a lot more life experience, and she was curious to find out if he was right.

He'd called it a soul promise. And while Paige didn't believe in forever in terms of human commitments, she did believe so, so strongly in existence after human death. No way she could see herself ever breaking a soul promise.

That was something that went far beyond forever.

Besides, he'd made a promise, too. He'd promised her that he'd watch over her siblings once he'd left earth.

Gabby and Ursula were so uptight. Worried all

the time about what bad could happen. They hadn't yet learned how to relax and let life just unfold. Instead, they were in a constant fight with it, trying to stay one step ahead of disaster in any given situation.

Being around them for any length of time exhausted her, though they kept in daily contact in a private social media group.

She hadn't told her sisters about inheriting a mansion.

Or about West.

They knew about the dogs, though. Stover leaving had been the day's post. They'd understood her tears. Had been able to relate to them. Which was why she'd chosen that particular topic to share…

Her thoughts froze midstream when she heard a footstep in the laundry room. Legs flying down to the mat so fast her ankles bumped hard against it, she sat up, back to the door, pressed her thighs tightly together and laid her forearms out, palms extended to the ceiling, her index fingers and thumbs connecting. The God finger connecting to the individual, personal self finger.

Her legs should be crossed lotus style if she wanted him to believe she was doing yoga, but no way she was opening her crotch to him at that or any moment.

She was banking on her assumption that Weston Thomas knew as much about yoga as she cared about spending her days looking at columns of numbers.

And prayed that he'd see her prayer position and quietly slip back into the ether.

Hard as a rock, Weston figured he'd probably never fully recover from the view he'd just had of Paige Thomas's crotch, barely concealed with pink fabric that had outlined some beautiful curves in such a thorough way.

He'd approached the kennel room softly, hoping that she'd be off to bed, and not wanting to wake all the dogs, or get them riled up.

Instead, her legs up as though she was giving birth, her hands clutching the arches of her feet to hold them there, was the most impactful hello he ever had or ever would receive. As quietly as he'd arrived, he'd backed up. Moving slowly enough that even the dogs who were awake didn't notice him.

Nor did their human companion.

His immediate thought had been to go back upstairs to his room, get to the computer and try to get some work done. He hadn't planned on taking Monday off, and he had a feeling after his talk with Lieberman that he was going to need the entire day to sort out his father's affairs.

And his lack of future affairs with the woman his father was somehow trying to tie him to.

He'd made it out to the kitchen before the stark

emptiness that had brought him downstairs in the first place struck again. He'd come down for Checkers.

And still wanted to take the dog upstairs with him. Paige had the other five to keep her company for the night. All he was asking for was the one old guy that his father had formally adopted.

He'd gone out for dinner. Had offered to get some for her, but she'd said she had stuff in the refrigerator. Standing in the kitchen he didn't see any sign that she'd used it.

And felt a little bad about that, too.

He didn't want her to think that she had to stay locked in the kennel, away from the rest of the house. Until Monday they had equal access. He needed to make certain he communicated that.

All of which had brought him back out to the laundry room, walking with exaggerated sound as he approached the kennel room a second time.

And stood there frozen, in awe of her beauty, as she sat, palms to the ceiling, praying.

The woman was an enigma. A thorn, an irritant, and a slice of otherworldly beauty, too. He wanted her gone. There was no doubt at all about that.

And yet…he was glad to have met her.

He stood silently, waiting. No way he'd interrupt her prayer time.

But the little poodle/bichon mix who didn't eat enough, Annie, noticed him standing there. And when he continued to stand, she stood, too, ears up, and started to growl. Weston squatted down at the first sign of disturbance, but the little pug, who was using a corner of the yoga mat, barked. Then the beagle did. And the skinny terrier, Abe, came running toward him, tail wagging. He glanced up from petting the dog to see Paige watching him.

She didn't look happy to have him there. But she didn't seem angry, either.

He didn't even want to think about the daggers she'd shoot his way if she knew he'd been there a few minutes earlier, too.

There were some things a decent guy kept to himself.

Including the ramifications of a healthy sex drive.

He'd have an easier time with that particular challenge if she'd put something on over that purple thing she was using for a top. It left more of her bare than it covered. And let him see, quite clearly, that her nipples were hard.

"I...wanted to fully acknowledge to you that I recognize your right to move freely about the house. You don't have to stay in the back room. There are plenty of nice spaces upstairs."

"I've actually never been up there," she said, standing and reaching for the skirt she'd had on earlier. Stepping into it.

He'd never known watching a woman put her

clothes on—rather than taking them off—could be so damned hot. Making him way too hot.

"And I'm perfectly happy downstairs for now," she continued. "At least until Monday. Once things are settled, then I'd like to see the whole place, and maybe pick a different room."

Another reference to him maybe not getting his father's house.

He wanted to remind her that she could very well be looking for another place to live on Monday, but held the words back. There was no point in antagonizing her further.

"I also came down to get Checkers," he said. The big old shepherd lay on a rug in front of the brown couch. He'd looked up, though.

He couldn't hear, but maybe his sense of smell told him someone else had entered the room? Or the ruckus of the other dogs had gotten through to him?

"I thought maybe he could sleep upstairs with me."

"There's no doggy door up there."

"I'll take him out before bed." He'd had a dog before. He knew how it worked. "And if he gets up in the night, I'll put him out again." He didn't want to have to make it clear that he wasn't asking. But he would if she pushed him.

He stared her down. She nodded. "He likes that rug. Maybe take that up with you. And a bowl of water," she added.

Because she just couldn't not get a word in, was that it? Or did she think him that selfish and incapable that he'd deny an old dog water all night?

Again, he held back his thoughts. Nodded. Went to the cupboard for one of the stack of clean bowls he'd seen there. Waiting for future rescues, he assumed. Helping himself to one, he approached Checkers, wondering, now that he'd taken his stance, if the dog would even come with him. It wasn't like he could call to him. Coax him.

If he'd have been smarter, he'd have grabbed a treat from the box he'd seen in the cupboard.

Paige watched his every move, of course.

Waiting for him to fail?

Or maybe just giving Weston the courtesy of letting him take his own path? A minute before he'd been edgy because she'd been instructing him. He couldn't have it both ways.

Whether he was cranky or not.

He didn't just kneel in front of Checkers, he sat. Dress pants on cement floor. Cement floor covered with a day's worth of dog hair. Didn't even bother him. He'd find a new dry cleaner soon enough. Placing his hand in front of the dog's nose, he let Checkers smell him. And then touched him under his chin, and lightly scratched his neck. It might have been a dozen years since he'd owned a pet, but some things you just didn't forget.

"Signing legal documents and joining our names legally doesn't have to mean any more than that."

Her words came softly. Interrupting his communion with a guy who was probably wiser than both of them.

"Come again?"

"If the will requires us to be married. We could go to the courthouse, get a license, go through the legalities. And then do the same in reverse." She'd dropped down to the mat again, had Erin on her lap.

"Get married and then divorced?"

She shrugged. "Just saying…if that's what it takes…"

She had a point. But left a huge problem hanging out there. "And, say we did that, who would get the mansion?"

Because he damn sure wasn't living there with her. He'd been certain of that before. But after seeing what he'd seen…

He got hard just thinking about it. And quickly thought of columns of numbers. Of a cold body of water filled with alligators, to deflate.

If she had an answer to his question, she didn't voice it. Probably a wise choice.

He stood up, tugging gently on Checkers's collar, and was surprised when the dog stood, and then, with urging in the form of taps on the head and hand motions, followed Weston to the door.

"Your dad used to take him upstairs with him at night."

Which maybe explained why Checkers was going with him so easily.

But something about her words, in her usual soft tones, was different. Deeper. Like she was telling him something important.

He hadn't known of Walter's habit. No one had told him.

And yet he'd had to come down and get the dog.

Probably just a coincidence. Or habit born from Rusty sleeping with Weston every night until Weston left for college. He still had nights that he missed the dog.

He had a feeling Paige was reading more into it than that. Trying to draw some kind of other-worldly connection.

He continued out of the room, leaving her to her ruminations.

But found them trailing behind him as he headed out the front door and into the luscious two acres of grass with his dad's old pup.

Chapter Six

Paige spent most of Sunday with the dogs. While she'd put all of her groceries away in the kitchen the day before, she opted to step out to eat rather than risk running into West. The couple minutes she'd seen him in the morning, during feed time, had sent her into overload.

She'd been standing there watching the dogs chomp, waiting for them to finish so she could take Annie into the laundry room and coax her to eat more than a bite, when West had come in looking like a sexy bedtime romp in thin cotton pants and a T-shirt, his short hair standing up, that shadow of beard back, and slippers on his feet.

"I haven't overslept in years," he'd told her, his voice still raspy from slumber. "Checkers woke me. He's been out." And as he'd moved to feed the big old dog, he'd continued with, "I'll take the evening feeding for all of them."

Her hope had been that he'd been so busy excusing himself he hadn't noticed her drooling over him. Hadn't seen the smile she'd been wearing. She'd wiped it off as soon as she'd become aware, a second or two into his speech.

"And I'll set my alarm in the morning. Just until I know for sure I'm back on track."

Those had been the words that had snatched her out of la-la land and had landed her firmly back on track. The morning referring to Monday morning. When they had shared appointments with an expert attorney. West was not a potential sex partner. He was her adversary. One who'd robbed her of peace of mind the night before. Who'd robbed her of her power over herself, something that just didn't happen.

Until she knew what she was up against with him, until she could actually do something about it, she had to keep her distance.

And, as with most things to which she put her mind, she did it very well. Perhaps with his assistance. He never came to the kennel—she never ventured out into the house—except when feeding time approached Sunday evening. Then she went into her room, listening to be sure he showed up to feed the dogs. She'd ventured out to the kitchen then, long enough to hear him talking to each animal, addressing them by name, and then, grabbing her keys, she'd left the premises. Treated herself to dinner at one of her favorite Mexican restaurants—takeout. And had eaten it at the lovely park a couple miles from Walter's property.

Checkers had been absent when she'd returned

to the dogs' room an hour later. And when he'd re-appeared early Monday morning, West was right behind him, in black dress pants, a white shirt, cuffs buttoned at the wrist, a black-and-white tie and shiny black dress shoes, with laces neatly tied.

She knew because she had to focus on those shoes for a second while she got her bearings. The man filled out dress clothes like the male dancers at Chippendales filled out dance belts.

She'd put on a magenta-and-white high-waist, ankle-length skirt, with a sleeveless button-down, tapered at the waist, and her dressiest flip-flops with the white straps and wedge bottoms. Feeling like a peddler at a fair next to him, she'd thought about pulling back her hair. Was glad she hadn't bothered. It wouldn't have made a difference.

After their joint meeting, Lieberman was going to be working for *her*. That was all that mattered. She had expert legal counsel on her side.

By the time she'd composed herself, West was already at the counter, bowls lined up. He'd failed to wash them the night before. She'd done it after she'd returned from dinner, but didn't point out the fact. If he noticed, he didn't say.

They served the dogs in total silence. And while he stood with the others, she took Annie into the laundry room and sat hand-feeding the timid animal. She didn't have half an hour or more to let Annie make peace with her bowl on her own.

West came through while she was still sitting with Annie, letting her know he'd see her at the lawyer's office, and continued on to the kitchen. She heard the coffeepot.

She'd already made her tea.

And when she made it back to the kennel room with Annie's half-empty bowl, she noticed the other five dog bowls lined up on a drying towel on the counter next to the sink.

When part of her started to melt at his show of consideration, she threw what ice she could on the matter. This man was determined to get everything right. Including figuring out before she did how to keep Walter's estate—and her ability to keep her soul promise to the old man—away from her.

He hadn't mentioned driving together to the meeting with Grant Lieberman. She'd have turned him down if he had. And was determined to get to the office before West did. No way she was walking in to find him already charming Grant into a guys-stick-together situation. She might lead with peace and joy, but she bore a core of steel when it came to the bottom line, taking care of her siblings, herself or the things she cared about. She might be the youngest in the family, and her sisters might think she needed to be watched over, protected, but she knew that the situation was completely the opposite. She'd recovered from the tragedy they hadn't witnessed far better than they had.

They needed her to be strong.

Her defenses sky-high, she walked into the room twenty minutes early, to find herself the first one there. And when West arrived, five minutes later, nodding to her from the doorway, and then taking the seat next to her along one side of the six-chair table, she'd come down a bit from her high horse.

She wasn't out to annihilate anyone. Most particularly not West. He was Walter's son. She'd grown to care about him, in an ethereal sense, over the months of learning about him through Walter's eyes.

And… "We both cared a great deal about your father," she said to him after seconds passed with neither of them saying so much as hello. "Whatever we're about to find out…we have to remember that they were his wishes."

His chin jutted. "I spent my entire youth pandering to him. Believing in his next great invention, only to have my trust betrayed. I learned through hard experience that you couldn't count on what he believed in. You couldn't count on a stable living environment. But you could always count on him admitting he was wrong. You could count on him to do his best to clean up his messes. And you could always count on a roof over your head and food on the table. The actual roof might change, or leak, the food might be canned soup for a week on end, but it was there."

She wasn't sure what to do with that. Walter's

wishes had a good chance, in West's mind, of being wrong?

But what about the rest of it? Walter cleaning up his messes? He was no longer on earth to do that.

But West was counting on his father to provide the roof over his head?

The man was fully capable of providing his own roof, but it wasn't about the financial provision. She got that much.

"I respected your father deeply and trusted him implicitly," she told him, countering his move to shed doubt on Walter's plan. She'd promised Walter, once he'd left money to the estate, not her, that she'd live in the house for the amount of time he'd designated as suitable enough for her to learn what he knew she'd want to know. One year. No matter what the will said, she intended to be an occupying owner of Walter's estate for at least that long.

"You were close with him."

"Very. In many ways he was like a father to me." In conjunction with the father she'd lost, not in replacement thereof...

West was not going to steer her off this course. He could try. She knew he would try.

He was determined, too.

But he absolutely could not win.

He was like a father to me.
As with many things about Paige Martinson, the

words threw Weston off course. He'd have been better able to digest her being his father's lover. That he could fit into his world.

But like a father? Weston was Walter's only child.

The territorial thought was childish. He recognized that. And still he felt the brunt of her words.

"He was like a father to you." It was statement, not question. Restatement, to be more precise. Clarification, if you would.

"Yes."

Nope, didn't sit any better the second time through. Was she angling to be a daughter-in-law posthumously? He wasn't marrying her. Or anyone. He'd fight for his inheritance in court. She had an attorney for a couple of months. He could afford one for life, even without his father's money.

"Yet you weren't at his funeral." The words came out a little like accusation.

"I said my goodbye to him the night he died. And I had to be here to take care of the dogs."

And his mood just continued to spiral downward. "You were with him the night he died?"

"Yes."

"Why am I only hearing this now?"

"You didn't ask any questions about him. About his last weeks. I was respecting your need to grieve in your own way. And trusted that you'd come to me when, or if, you were ready to hear more. Even if you didn't know he and I had become good friends, you'd have known I was at the house every day because of the dogs."

He saw red. And then blue. An ocean of turbulent blue. Emotion surged from his heart to his throat, pricked behind his lids.

Right there in the attorney's office.

He'd blame her for it, accuse her of trying to put him off his game at the crucial moment. But he was the one who'd brought up doubt when she'd been trying to lay a groundwork of peace and open-mindedness for the meeting ahead. And he was the one who'd first mentioned her closeness with his father.

And he didn't completely hate her answer. He was comforted to know that Walter hadn't died alone. Or with strangers.

He just hated that he hadn't been there. That he hadn't even been given the chance. That his father hadn't told him his heart was failing.

That he hadn't had a chance to give his dad his birthday present.

If it weren't for the stakes on the table, Weston would have stood up and walked out. Excusing himself as he did so, of course.

As it was, he was prevented from making things any more difficult for himself by the entry of the attorney neither one of them had met.

Grant Lieberman seemed easygoing enough,

bringing a kind smile into the room with him rather than the load of tension Weston had anticipated. The man was younger than he'd expected, forty at the most, and looked each of them straight in the eye as he introduced himself. The light-skinned Black man had a firm, reassuring grip and took charge of the meeting immediately.

"My intent is to read the will to you in its entirety first, so that we're all on the same page, and then I'll do my best to answer questions. After this meeting, I will be available only to Ms. Martinson on this matter, and my colleague, Diane Gale, is standing by to speak with you, Mr. Thomas, should you desire her immediate services. This is all by direction from the late Mr. Thomas, senior, and is written into the will."

Weston listened to the lawyer read, hearing his father in every word, waiting. His dad had been so certain Weston should let himself fall in love again after Mary's death. That Weston was wrong to deprive himself of the joy of getting married. It would be just like Walter to invent a circumstance to somehow make that happen. Trying to get Weston to believe in the impossible.

And wholly unfair to Paige Martinson that she'd be a pawn in Walter's scheme. Weston was having a hard time figuring that one out. His father didn't use people…

"I do hereby devise and bequeath…" The language went on, official listings and legal land and property descriptions. Paige didn't move. He could feel the warmth of her next to him, even through his shirt sleeve.

And then, there it was…one paragraph that left him…speechless.

It took a second for the words to fully sink in for Weston. He was a guy who computed facts and now he had them.

Such as they were.

"We don't have to get married." Paige's voice broke into his thoughts.

"In order for us to keep the house each of us has to live in it for a period no less than one year," Weston said out loud. As though hearing facts in his own voice would somehow give him more understanding. "And whoever stays in the house for the entirety of that period gets the house permanently."

"That's correct." The lawyer answered with a factual calm that didn't in any way acknowledge the impossibility of the situation.

Weston tried to point it out to him. "So, in essence, we could be living with each other for the rest of our lives."

With a raised hand, Lieberman said, "Or, you could live in the same house for one year, after which you maintain joint ownership for the rest of your lives, with either of you having the right to move, or stay, as you wish.

"In the event that either of you chooses not to remain in the home or treat it as a main residence for the next year, the entirety of the estate automatically reverts to the one who did stay. However, if that remaining one of you then vacates within the year, the estate goes to the national dog rescue foundation named in the will."

Yep. He'd been getting it right. "And this is legally binding." Weston attempted one more time to help the lawyer see sense.

"Absolutely. You each have the choice to accept or reject the terms of the will. Walter made provisions for every scenario he could think of."

Like the canine one. The dogs stayed with the house. Checkers permanently. The rescue operation permanently, too, though not the individual dogs themselves. And the human occupants had to be willing to continue the rescue operation, caring for the dogs themselves on a regular basis, or lose their inheritance.

Walter had specified the number of nights per month that each of the beneficiaries must sleep in the house—twenty-five—and that both must claim the home as their current permanent residence.

And he'd even given stipulations for the handling of household responsibilities and had already established a household account bearing enough money to last the year. They were to both be privy to all household bills paid and were joint signatories on the account.

No major household repairs or changes were to be made without consent from both parties.

He'd allowed them one month from the reading of the will to begin permanent occupancy—Lieberman had pointed out that the month was meant to give them both a chance to move from their current homes and positions, if necessary. He'd looked at Weston as he'd delivered that part of his remarks.

"Do we have to wait the month before the year starts?" he asked, just to be aware of all the facts, not because he was at all intending to simply abide by the ludicrous will.

"No. The month was just an option if you needed it."

"So it can be backdated to Friday?" Paige asked, as though the two days, to say nothing of the month, were a real issue. As though she was on board with the preposterous plan.

"As long as you both have spent the past two nights in the home."

"Why not just go back further than that?" Weston asked. "We only have to spend twenty-five of thirty days this month in the home. So, really we could go back another five days…"

He was being facetious. Because he had nothing else at the moment. He felt…trapped. In some kind of amusement park where there was so much excitement and beauty and promise, but there was no electricity to light the place up or run the rides.

Both Lieberman and Paige were looking at him. "I'm sorry," he said, fully meaning the words. "I just... Can't anyone else see how bizarre this is?"

"It's the most unusual will I've ever seen, I'll give you that," the attorney said. "But I can assure you, as will my colleague, Diane, that it's also airtight."

He shook his head. It couldn't be. Nothing was that perfect. And most certainly not a single one of his father's many failed inventions. But there'd been that one exception. The filtering bottle cap. That success had been stupendous.

Was still bringing in royalties beyond anything Weston could ever have imagined in his black-and-white world.

But that cap had been a fluke. The exception that proved the rule.

Wasn't it?

"Weston and I spoke briefly yesterday about the state of Walter's mental competency at the time the will was drawn up. I see here, by the date, that it was after he'd started on his regimen of medications. Is there..."

Weston sat up, impressed by his beneficiary mate, not only for bringing up a potentially difficult topic so he didn't have to, but for not pointing out that he was the one who'd mentioned the idea the day before. But Lieberman was already shaking his head.

Folding his hands together, Grant leaned forward, addressing Paige. "Did you ever notice any signs of a lack of clarity in him?"

She shook her head.

"And you spent a lot of time with him these past few months, seeing him at least briefly every day."

She nodded.

The attorney threw his hands outward and shrugged. "There's your best defense witness."

"But…" Surely the man of the law didn't expect them just to leave it at that…

Lieberman's expression appeared more sympathetic than anything else as he addressed Weston. "Your father, thinking of this very eventuality, submitted to a court-appointed psychological exam before the signing of the will. Trust me, it will stand up in any court in this country."

There had to be some other way…

"Like I said, either of you are free, at any time, to leave. The stipulations only apply if you want the inheritance."

Of course he wanted it. They were talking about his father's home. His dogs. The last years of his life. The residual of his life's work. Weston would give up the money in a heartbeat, but no way could he turn his back on any of the other things.

He glanced at Paige.

And, clear as day, knew what he had to do.

He'd pay her. However much she wanted, every dime of his father's royalties as soon as the money belonged to him, every month for the rest of his life, if that was what it took. She could buy any house she wanted. Another mansion if that was her heart's desire. Enough that she could build another rescue kennel.

Based on what he'd learned over the weekend, it wasn't like there was a lack of dogs needing homes. That way they'd be saving twice as many animals. That would make her happy, too.

He just needed to speak with her alone to work out the details. And then she could run things by Lieberman—her attorney alone now.

Problem solved, he stood. Thanked the lawyer. And showed himself out.

Chapter Seven

She didn't have to get married! There'd been no such stipulation. Not even a hint of one. And, true to form, Walter had kept his word to her. She only had to live in the house for a year for it to be hers, though West had to do the same.

Paige was weak with relief as she drove her older-model, but pristine-condition, SUV out of the lawyer's office parking lot.

The idea of making vows before a justice and signing papers making those vows legally binding had just not sat well with her. Seemed duplicitous on a soul level and that wasn't the way she rolled.

And there'd been no way she could enter into a marriage with an honest intent to stay there until she died.

That wasn't her way, either.

So, yeah, there was a bit of a wrench in the plan with West also being in residence, but the place was huge. There was enough square footage for three families to live in and never see each other.

For the first time since Walter's death, she could

feel a bit of a real smile coming on. A note of honest anticipation rising up inside her.

Whether Walter's plan proved successful or not, whether she gained any understanding or depth from the year of owning the place where she lived, she was still at the start of a new chapter and it came with dogs!

Maybe…just maybe…she'd be able to write in a way that honored Walter to the fullest. To show the world the deep value of the man—value that had absolutely nothing to do with material things.

She hoped West was feeling a measure of comfort as well. Things hadn't turned out exactly as he'd expected, but he was keeping the house.

And didn't have to get married.

She heaved another mammoth sigh of relief as she pulled onto the street that led to the outlying Atlanta area of huge properties where Walter had found his bliss. She'd been so torn about that marriage thing.

And hoped, had it been a stipulation, that she'd have made the right choice. Keeping a soul promise was paramount.

And living with honest and pure intent was, too.

It felt good, pulling past the circular front drive where, until Saturday, she'd always parked, and continuing back to the garage she'd taken over as her own two days before. There were four double garages. She had one. If West had a problem with her choice, they could talk about it.

West.

She had no idea if he was home yet or not.

Was trying to pretend not to notice the trepidation she felt at the thought of seeing him again. As much as she wanted to be alone, she didn't want him to leave.

The thought was as confusing to her as the rest of the past two days had been.

West was Walter's son. He belonged in Walter's home. Most particularly because he wanted to be there. She just had to reassure him that he'd never know she was around.

They were smart, independent people.

They could make Walter's plan work.

As eager as she was to climb the wide winding staircase and visit the five-thousand-square-foot second floor, to find what glories awaited there, she went to see the dogs first, most eager to assure them that all was fine in their world.

That they were permanently secure.

Any that weren't adopted just stayed. The practice had been part of Walter's operation from day one. While the dogs might not understand the details of the concept, she worked every day to show them that they wouldn't be hurt or abandoned again. There would always be meals when they were hungry, and their days would consist of companionship, kindness and love.

And what happened to them beyond the year she would remain?

The question came to her as she entered the laundry room—and thought of hand-feeding Annie that morning.

Dogs weren't expected to live more than ten to eighteen years, depending on the breed. She'd known, going in, that she'd likely be telling them goodbye and was prepared to do so.

But Walter's dogs…

So, any that weren't adopted, and that West didn't want, she'd take with her. Somehow.

The idea wasn't a full plan yet. She didn't quite know how it would work, having canine companions as she went off to whatever her next chapter would be, but she had time to figure it out.

The thought was mostly wiped from her mind as she entered the kennel room and saw West there already, on *her* couch, with Abe on one side of him and Erin on the other. Checkers lay at his feet. Buddy was off on a dog bed in the corner. And Annie and Darcy were both sitting up, watching West, giving Paige the impression that she'd just interrupted an important meeting or something.

He must have been talking aloud, until he'd heard her come through. It wasn't like she'd been quiet. She hadn't expected anyone but the dogs to be there and she liked them to know she was on her way in. Buddy had heart palpitations sometimes when people descended on him too quickly.

"I wanted to get with you right away, before you make any plans, or tell too many people about your inheritance." West spoke as soon as she appeared in the doorway.

"You could have called me. We could have met for breakfast or lunch or something." Someplace neutral to both of them. Away from the house.

And less intimate.

With a human audience, even if just in the form of other diners and employees.

Not that he didn't have every right to be in the kennel. Or on that older, more used of the two couches.

It was just the room was one she thought of as hers—except at feeding times when she now knew to expect him to appear.

And the couch…her comfort place…

But he was right to get down immediately to the business of sharing the property. Like the garage. She shouldn't have just chosen hers arbitrarily. They should discuss everything with each other first.

Even if the will hadn't stipulated as much, it was only respectful and fair to do so.

Maybe she could claim the sofa he was invading as hers. He could permanently have and use the brown one. It was newer, nicer and in a more shaded part of the room.

Feeling too much like she was standing onstage in a spotlight, she perched on the edge of the brown couch.

"Your father bought this couch for Stover. So he'd have a place of his own to stretch out. He never used it, though." And the dog was gone.

To a happy home.

Maybe the couch should be, too. If no one there wanted to use it. They could get a sectional with all the various pieces that would make it like a big king-size bed with arms and a back.

She opened her mouth to suggest the idea, but closed it again. She didn't need to be having any kind of bed talk with Weston Thomas.

Not now or in the future.

If they were going to share the house successfully, and painlessly, they had to have some boundaries. Some unspoken ones that would be clear just by avoiding certain topics.

Like beds. And gorgeous male bodies.

There was a lot she could give him, though. Just like the tidbit about Walter buying the couch. That kind of history existed all over the house and she was the sole keeper of it all. It felt good, knowing she had deep value to contribute, comfort to offer Walter's only offspring.

"I'm prepared to offer you a monthly sum, in the

amount of the bottle cap royalties, in exchange for you physically vacating the property, which would then break your stipulation in the will and make the estate my sole property."

Her hissed-in breath wasn't purposeful. Planned. Or avoidable.

She'd overestimated Weston Thomas. Given him too much credit for being the type of man who'd care about the desires of the man who'd had the will drawn up, not just about the letter of the law.

The type of man who'd honor and respect his father's last wishes.

"It's my father's home. It makes sense that I'd be the one to stay," he continued as though he hadn't noticed her distress.

The way her hands were suddenly shaking was an embarrassment to her. She shoved them under her thighs.

She wasn't only surprised. Put off.

She was…hurt.

And insulted.

If her glance didn't let him know that, the icy tone in her voice would. "I don't want Walter's money. I never did."

"No, I didn't mean…" He sat forward, frowning, a look of sincerity lighting those striking green eyes. She wanted to shock that look right off his face and… "I profusely apologize for the way that sounded," he went on. "I know you aren't a gold digger, or anything remotely resembling one. I'm just saying, this house, every possession in it, the way it's all arranged or put away…it's all my father. But he wanted you to have a place like it so I'll pay for you to have one. You'll have enough money to build a second kennel. Think about it, two rooms will be twice the dogs rescued."

She loved the thought. Twice the dogs.

"We could build a second kennel here, with separately fenced outdoor access, just like this one. You could take care of one and I'd do the other," she said, running with the only thing he'd said that she could accept. A second kennel. It was a great idea. Doable. "I'd want it to be a fully separate second room, though. The idea here is for them to feel at home. Part of a family. Not just a bunch of animals shoved together because there's nowhere else for them to go." Darcy sat in front of her, put his paw on her knee. He had to be sensing her tension and she felt awful about that. Put out a hand to stroke the white star on his chest and she relaxed a bit as his gaze became slumberous.

"That's not what I meant."

Of course it wasn't. She knew that. But… "Your father could have bought me a place if that's what he'd wanted. He wanted me here. In this home. And you aren't the only one with emotional attachments to claim here," she asserted, her determination growing in leaps and bounds. A couple months before, she'd been refusing to have anything to do with Walter's desire to leave his home to her. "I know the history of so many things, like this couch here, for instance. But beyond things... I've got over a year's worth of memories within these walls." Way more than he did, though she wasn't so unkind as to drive that point any deeper. "And I have a bond with the soul who left them here."

Maybe that last bit was too much for him. Too out there. She didn't care, though.

"We can't live together."

A tingle shot down between her legs, the way he said that. The picture his words brought to mind. While she tamped down a sense of excitement— a simple anticipation of the unknown, she told herself—he continued.

"You don't seriously think we're both going to stay here."

"It's what your father wanted, Weston." He'd asked that she not use the shortened version of his name and at the moment she needed to give him what she could. "We're talking about Walter's dying wish. I don't know why. But I know I want to do what I can to find out. To give him a shot at being successful in this last endeavor. It's only for a year. I can handle a year. Can't you?"

He shook his head. Ran a hand from his forehead back, wiping a dry brow—one that clearly didn't need to be wiped. And in spite of herself, her heart went out to him.

"Think of it like a business, West. *Weston*," she quickly corrected, almost desperate now to keep Walter's wishes intact.

He didn't want her there alone. If he had, he'd have left her as sole owner of the home.

"We're co-owners of a business. We each have emotional attachments to the business itself, but our relationship is just a partnership to keep the business functioning successfully."

He watched her. Taking encouragement from his silence, thinking she might be getting through to him, she added, "You're just starting up two businesses instead of one."

He sat, hands stilled, dogs on either side of him.

"It's only for a year." She pressed the advantage.

"No, it's not, Paige." She heard his tone of voice and knew, even before he stood up, that she should have quit while she was ahead. "It's for a lifetime. If we both stay here for the year, we both own the property for the rest of our lives."

Yes, but…her promise to Walter had only been for a year.

"So, how about this…" She stood, too, trembling again as they met eye to eye, only inches between one other. "How about if, after the year is up, I agree to sell you my half of the estate?" She wouldn't take his money, even then. But had an idea that unless she kept things strictly business they might both lose everything Walter had tried to leave them.

All the things they didn't yet know. Things his greater life experience had shown him.

West frowned, seemingly more from confusion than anything else. As though he was trying to form a full assessment of her.

She wished him luck with that.

She'd been living with herself for a lifetime and she hadn't yet figured everything out.

"Look at this way," she said, fighting for something she didn't even understand yet. "If I'm wrong, if Walter Thomas was an inventor whose imagination drove him to a lifetime filled with all but one dead end, if the will is just his last failure, then so be it. But don't you think his chance for one last success is worth a year of our lives?"

He shoved his hands in his pockets. Shook his head.

And her heart sank.

"You're weird, you know that?"

She shrugged, not really caring what the world thought of her. She'd escaped that kind of thinking at eleven.

If she'd believed the world, then she'd have been no more than a girl to be pitied above all else. A child who had undergone a horrifically sad experience that would define her forever.

Darcy nudged her thigh, hard. Reaching for his

paw, she soaked up the warmth he'd offered, taking up the spot West had vacated on her couch. Then she pulled Annie onto her lap.

She wasn't going anywhere. Whether she did it with West, as Walter wanted most, or alone, she was going to keep her promise.

"Like a business, huh?"

The couch sank beside her and she glanced over at the man who was making life so much more difficult than she needed it to be.

She wasn't giving up any more of her thoughts to him.

"You really think we can make it work?"

"For a year." She had to make that point clear. And was suddenly way more nervous than she'd been since finding West Thomas in the foyer of Walter's home Saturday morning.

"I'll go call Diane Gale and get something in writing to solidify our agreement. We live in the house together, as co-owners, as my father stipulated, for one year. And then, when you leave of your own free will, you agree to sell me your interest in the estate."

Giving Annie a hug, kissing the top of the dog's head, Paige gave herself a moment to breathe. And then looked over at West.

"Can we agree on the financial terms of the sale at the end of the year?"

With a slight head tilt, he studied her.

"I just don't want a dollar amount in the contract." Because she wasn't going to be put in a position where she was forced to take his money to buy her freedom.

It only took a second, and the shuttered look to come over his face, for her to realize how her caveat could sound to him, though. As though she wanted to be able to hold him hostage to more than her fair share…

"Unless it says something like 'an amount not to exceed such and such amount of dollars,'" she quickly added. She could sign that.

Because she could be true to the agreement and still sell him her half of the estate for a dollar.

He named an amount that was far too generous. She didn't care. Her future request couldn't exceed that amount. Nothing said it couldn't be lower. And so she nodded.

He did, too.

Then he smiled at her.

Her body melted.

And she wondered what in the hell she'd let herself in for.

Chapter Eight

Weston was on the phone with his Sierra's Web attorney, Diane, within minutes of his conversation with Paige. He wasn't going to relax until the agreement was locked up tight with legal bindings.

His father wanted her there. Paige's presence at the mansion, her co-ownership, Weston's own part in the scheme—it was his father's dying wish.

It had taken Paige putting it bluntly to get him to see that.

He'd been so consumed with the idea of a hare-brained marriage scheme...

And yet, that one-year stipulation that he and Paige occupy the residence...that wasn't the lifetime to which Walter had constantly nagged him to commit.

So maybe he'd been so busy keeping his defenses up against the old man, so as not to be disappointed again, by Walter or life in general, that he'd failed to see what was right there in front of him.

Was there something else he'd missed? He'd always taken himself for a good listener in general, but in particular where his father was concerned.

He'd sit for hours and pay attention to the nitty-gritty details of the next great invention, which all too often would fail.

Five minutes after he dialed Diane's number, leaving a message for her to call at her earliest convenience, she called him back.

And two minutes after that he was seeking out Paige again.

She wasn't in with the dogs. Checkers was there, though, and sat up when Weston entered. Which was why he ended up outside with all six animals. You couldn't take one over another.

And he didn't want Checkers to think that he didn't notice his hello.

He walked with them all, looking at the grounds as he did so. Thinking he'd like to open up the dog yard another acre at least. And plant some trees.

Male dogs liked trees.

Rusty had.

Checkers did.

In the front yard the night before, Checkers had gone straight for a tree to lift his leg.

Maybe if Buddy had a tree outside, he'd use the doggy door more often rather than going on the floor.

He needed to make some calls. Find a fence guy. And an arborist who could get him at least one mature tree. And then others that would grow with time.

Time. Would he be there long enough for time to grow trees?

And would Paige agree to having them planted in the first place, if he *was* still there?

Abe danced around his feet, while the little pug, Erin, let herself back inside. He had their names down. Knew who had to get what flea and intestinal parasite medications.

He knew that Checkers snored louder than Walter ever had.

And he had no idea what he was doing, standing out in his father's yard in Georgia late on a Monday morning, thinking about his pets.

And with no idea where the next hours were going to take him.

He needed to know.

His well-being hinged on him knowing.

Four of the six dogs had gone back inside. Just Buddy and Checkers were still out, and Weston, knowing they regularly let themselves in and out , headed in through the people door just down from the doggy door, and went in search of Paige.

He'd calmed down some.

He could let her know in a respectful, business-like way that her plan wasn't going to work.

He just didn't know what he could do to make his way in the world in which his father had trapped him.

Or how he was going to manage to have another conversation with the woman who was blowing his life to smithereens without her also figuring out how much she was getting to him.

Paige was lying in the middle of the most exquisitely soft and welcoming green-bedspread-covered mattress, gazing out the French doors to the balcony beyond them. Her wireless earbuds were playing new age harp with an orchestral background as she soaked up the happiness, when she felt something touch her foot.

"Ahhhh!" Her alarm-filled scream completely drowned out the peaceful melodies that had been soothing her soul, and the shard of electric fear was still coursing through her when she saw the source of the interruption.

By that time, she'd also pulled both feet up to her knees and was half sitting—giving West an intimate view up her skirt. Shoving her heels down abruptly and yanking down the garment, she watched him glance from her thighs to her face.

Then back up a couple of steps before turning around and exiting the room.

Thoughts about staying right where she was tempted her for about ten seconds. Until she remembered the part where she'd have to see him again, relatively soon, and every day for a lot of the next year.

"Weston?" she called, barely remembering to get out the last syllable. She pulled out the earbuds, shoving them into the pocket of her skirt next to her phone, as she slid into the flip-flops she'd left beside the bed and went after him.

His head disappeared around the far corner of the long hallway, in the direction of the west staircase.

"West!"

He paused, glancing down the skinniest of the three staircases she'd discovered leading to the second floor, as though he was judging his chances of getting away from her.

And then turned back. "I apologize. I shouldn't have interrupted."

"Of course you should have. I was lollygagging. Did you make the appointment for us to sign the year-end document?" She supposed that was why he'd sought her out. That document seemed to be the only lifeline he could find to hang on to.

He wouldn't look her in the eye. Part of her kind of liked that. Liked that an intimate sight of her unsettled him a bit.

The rest of her was ashamed of herself.

"I'm sorry I scared you."

She nodded. "You had no idea I had earbuds in."

"I probably should have figured it out when I called out to you and you didn't answer."

He'd called her name?

And when she hadn't responded, he had come in to check on her?

What a sweet thing to have done.

Making him uneasy was a tad bit amusing. In a fun kind of way. But having him being genuinely nice and looking out for her…she didn't need that kind of complication.

"I'm assuming Diane's given you a time to expect the agreement to be ready?" She was all business now. Getting her priorities firmly back in place.

Yeah, the room she'd chosen as her own was lovely beyond her wildest dreams. A perfect grown-princess kind of room.

But it was only hers for a year, assuming he agreed that the room was hers. Just like she'd have a chance to weigh in on whatever room he'd chosen for himself.

Anything else would come with more baggage for her to carry.

"There isn't going to be an agreement." His tone filled the spacious, wood-floored hallway with foreboding.

Smoothing her foot over the side edge of the maroon brocade runner, she asked, "Why not?"

"Remember those addendums that Lieberman told us about?"

She had a copy of them, as did West. "Yeah." Her heart sank at the frustration he emanated, but even more at the somewhat lost expression he wore.

He was not only an unhappy man at the moment, but he also seemed depleted. As though he was losing hope.

And she was being fanciful again. Just because she lived life knowing that hope for endless new possibilities was always there didn't mean that others did the same.

"Just as Lieberman advised, the addendums further define the stipulations in the will. One of which states that our joint residence here must be without any other living arrangements made by either one of us during the first year. Any agreements made between us to end our current situation or negotiate the future during this first year would void the will and the estate goes to charity, meaning the charity can keep it and use it, or sell it."

The estate going to charity didn't sound like a horrible thing to her.

Once she'd kept her soul promise.

But it sounded horrible when she thought of Weston losing his father's home. The home he'd told Lieberman he was planning to live in for the rest of his life.

The idea gave her the heebie-jeebies—being trapped in one place for life—but, if that was what he wanted, she wanted it for him. And figured Walter would, too.

And waited for the other shoe to drop.

West put his hands in his pockets—something

he seemed to do a lot. And then turned as if to head back downstairs.

"Wait," she called him back. "That's it? We can't negotiate another agreement for a year?"

"Yes." The succinct word came with an equally sharp head nod.

"So what's the problem, Weston?" She shook her head, pushing long strands back behind her elbow when they came falling forward. And then shrugged. "We know our plan. The day the year is up, we find a title company and get the sale done."

He stood there, watching her.

"We can keep a calendar on the refrigerator in the kennel," she said, picking up steam as relief sailed through her. "We cross off each day at night, kind of ceremonially, as we do the last feeding, with the last day of our year circled in gold! I've got some star stickers I can put around it."

"And what if you change your mind and decide you want to stay?"

She chuckled, then, seeing his completely serious face, sobered. "If you knew me better, you'd know that the chances of that are less than of hell freezing over. But even if the sky fell in, we survived and I had some kind of epiphany and felt like I had to be here, I'd still sell you my half."

"You can't possibly know that."

"Oh, yes I can," she told him, as dead serious as

he was. And probably more determined, though he might find that hard to believe.

He shook his head. "You sound like my dad, always so certain that he's right, up until he discovers the flaw in his thinking, and then, after taking accountability for the fallout of the one particular failure, just goes on to the next grand plan, unaware of the others his enthusiasm affected. Or how the failure affected them."

He stopped talking abruptly, as if realizing what he'd said and regretting it hugely. Once again, he turned away.

"West?" Once again she called him back. Purposely leaving off the last syllable of his name. Again.

He'd just given her an insight Walter never had. The inventor's tales of his son's enthusiasm for every project, for West's apparently mutual interest and subsequent input, had been wonderful to hear.

Walter had never said, and she'd never thought to ask, how West had reacted when they'd failed. She'd assumed, like his father, he'd shrugged off the failure and moved on to the next great adventure.

As she'd have done.

And maybe she should have seen that Walter's perception was based on his own interpretation of events and might not reflect Weston's truth at all.

His gaze was hooded as he watched her, though

he hadn't turned fully back. He had one foot half off the top step.

"I can be sure because I made the promise. And I don't break my promises." He didn't look any further convinced. "We don't know each other well, but something you can learn about me right now—I live my life with an eye to preserving my next one. My keeping my word to you has nothing to do with you. Or this estate. I'm not going home with something like stealing a man's inheritance away from him on my scorecard. And I'm not taking broken vows with me, either. Not the kind of thing I intend to saddle myself with."

Frowning, he cocked his head as he turned back toward her. "Your next life? Going home? I didn't realize you had a home."

"Home. When I die. The next life."

He didn't look as shocked as she'd thought he might. In her experience, not many people her age lived with an eye to dying someday. She envied them that. Living without a critical awareness of death.

She'd been that innocent once, too.

"It's just something I believe in, deep in my core," she continued. He'd seemed open to what she'd said, and the more they understood each other, the happier the next twelve months would be. "I don't know where or what the next life is. I don't have any real concept of it right now, but I know that it's there."

When he still remained silent, she added, "And hey, if I'm wrong, if I'm just some flighty woman who has her head in the clouds, who am I hurting by keeping my promises?"

"I don't think you're flighty."

The flood of warmth that suffused her, and pooled down low, might convince him otherwise.

"You're different than anyone I've ever met, but I have no intention of underestimating you."

She took that as a compliment. And wasn't letting him off the hook. "We have an agreement," she told him. "It was binding the second we agreed upon it. Paperwork is for the rest of the world. And we'll see to that when we can. Agreed?"

She couldn't afford to have the year fail. And he needed to know that, after a year, he'd have the place to himself. Just as she needed to know she'd be free to go.

The effects of his slow grin slid from her eyes to her toes and back again.

"Agreed," he told her. And then added, "I can see why my father chose you to write his memoirs."

She wanted to ask what he meant, but her tongue was glued to the roof of her mouth by dryness.

"I take it you've chosen your room," he said then, nodding down the hall toward the door they'd both so recently, and awkwardly, exited.

One at a time.

"I have." Technically, he could disagree, just as she could challenge his choice to bed down, but their point was to get along without having to be in constant contact. Which meant…giving the other space to make choices and trusting each other to keep each other's comforts and wishes in mind when doing so. He'd chosen his room without her input or agreement. He'd gone upstairs to bed, showered, which meant he'd chosen a place to do so.

And her room was on a completely different hallway, the one furthest from his. Not far from the top of the big winding staircase in the middle of the house.

"Have you looked at all of the others?"

She hadn't looked at any of the others. She had fallen in love with the first room. "No."

"Our current agreement didn't make any mention of the contents of the home. As far as I'm concerned, you'll have the right to take half of what's here with you when you go, so I suggest we go through it all together."

She traveled light, but he didn't need to know that. "Or we could each take a certain number of rooms and report back," she replied. She'd loved Walter. There might be a thing or two she'd like to have.

"Nothing against you, or as a sign of any lack of trust in you, but I'd like to go through it all together.

Everything here, my father put it together, chose it, placed it. I just want to…see it all."

So did she. And… "While I haven't been up here before now, I've heard about a lot of the rooms, and know stories about some of the furnishings," she offered.

She'd be a good thing in his life, not a sore spot.

Because that was how she rolled.

Not because she wanted him to like her, she insisted to herself.

Chapter Nine

Weston wanted to get through the main rooms on the two upstairs hallways they'd be using immediately so he'd have no more reason to venture into her hallway, and he wouldn't have to worry about her in his. Separate sleeping quarters, without any trespassing, was mandatory for his peace of mind.

The place where one gave up consciousness, where one got naked, posed the most danger to their current situation. Because it was when one was doing those things that one was most vulnerable.

Or so he'd determined. He could almost convince himself they were sharing an apartment complex with a communal kitchen, or maybe a college dormitory with only two residents.

Maybe he'd eat out while she was there. A year wasn't that long. Three hundred and sixty-five days. There had to be more than 365 restaurants in the Atlanta area. He could try one a day and not even come close to knowing the city's culinary offerings as well as he did those of his small Ohio hometown. It boasted a total of four sit-down restaurants. Including the coffee shop on Main Street. He'd eaten at all of them more times than he could count.

Since they were already in her hallway, they started their inventory there. With the door at the end. A linen closet.

Among the extra bed sheets and blankets, Weston recognized the comforter that used to be on his parents' bed when he was little. He'd forgotten it. And his action figure sheets were still there, too. Stunned, he stared for a moment.

He'd had no idea his father had kept them. Knew the fact that he had mattered.

And reclaimed them, meaning he spoke for them as his.

Other than those sheets and the one comforter, neither of them claimed the rest of the linens. It would all remain where and as it was for the time being. A linen closet was the place to store linens, not his bedroom. It wasn't like he'd be using the twin bed little boy sheets.

"Your dad said you were three when your mother died of kidney failure."

He'd just put back the comforter, the last thing to return to the closet shelf.

"Yeah." He nodded as he said the word. Closed the door. Turned to the next room down the hall.

"He said that she'd been told she shouldn't have kids, that it could exacerbate her chronic kidney problem, but she didn't tell your dad that until it was too late."

In a regular life, her words would have hit him upside the head, and he'd have responded by demanding that this conversation cease and never happen again. Or an ending of the relationship. But there was nothing regular about the life he was living.

And the woman…he didn't like not knowing what she knew about him.

Still…

Was there anything Walter hadn't told her? He'd thought the memoir was about Walter Thomas, the inventor. Sure, there'd be a brief mention of his personal life, but…

"He also said that she never regretted the choice." Paige's words followed him into a generic-looking bedroom/bathroom suite. "He said that she was happier those three years with you than she'd ever been. And that she would never have been as happy if she'd lived another twenty years without a child."

He'd heard that, too. From his father. And others. He'd kind of always thought the words had been spoken for his benefit. A planned story to ease any guilt he might have felt for being an indirect cause of his mother's death.

But if that was the case…there'd have been no reason for Walter to tell Paige about it. He could have just said Barbara Thomas had died of kidney failure.

He opened drawers. Tall chest first. Was it possible the words said to comfort him were actually true?

The idea lingered. Something he'd bring out again.

When he was alone.

He wasn't engaging in her intrusion into his private life. His father had given her access. Weston had not.

"He also said that she said many times, near the end, that if she had a chance to make the same choice, to have you, she'd do it all over again."

Yeah, he knew that, too. And the drawers were all empty. He moved to the dresser, still not responding to Paige's ongoing chatter.

"She begged him to forgive her."

He hadn't known that. He stopped, fingers midway in their reach to the next handle, turned, studied her as she bent to nightstand drawers, busy finding nothing, as she talked. "Forgive her for what?"

He broke his promise to himself to give her no response.

"Surely he didn't blame her for having faulty kidneys?"

Standing, Paige looked over at him, her flowing hair and flowing clothes giving her an earthy but angelic appearance that made it difficult for him to breathe.

"He didn't blame her for anything," she said softly. A declaration that rang completely true to him. His father had never exhibited any bitterness over his mother's death.

Sadness, yes. There'd been moments of deep grief through the years. But the moments passed without even a hint of anger.

"He was always thankful for the years they had together. Said that his time with her was a blessing that lifted him even after her death," he said, frowning. "So why did she think she needed forgiveness? For not telling him the pregnancy was a life risk?"

It was the only thing that made sense, and it was rebutted with a shake of Paige's head. She pushed back the hair that fell forward with those gentle feminine fingers. A gesture he was beginning to associate with her.

An action that only someone who knew her would know was habitual.

"She wanted him to forgive her for seeming to love you more than him. For putting your birth first, even though it meant losing years with her husband."

As his mother seemed to become more alive within Paige's voice, he knew his own regret. He would like to have more than just vague memories.

"She said that she'd known she'd be dying first, and she wanted to leave him with a piece of them, of their union, that would carry on into the world even when they were both gone. She didn't want to leave him alone. She hoped he'd forgive her for making the choice selfishly. Choosing what she wanted for him. For not asking him what he wanted"

With a little more force than intended, Weston shut the empty drawer he'd just pulled open. Swallowed and could feel the trembling in his chin from muscles clenched so tightly.

Going through the rooms of the house together with her had been a bad idea.

An atrocious idea.

One of his worst.

"He told her that, had he known, he would have honored her choice."

He stood, facing the dresser, needing to get to the door, and out. His feet didn't move.

"I don't think he was just saying that to comfort her. I think he was being honest with her, and I've thought about that a lot. Your dad might have spent a lot of his time conjuring up impossible dreams, but maybe that's because when it came to the real stuff of life...he already had all the answers."

When tears sprang to his eyes, Weston was through the door, and he didn't stop moving until he'd taken the stairs, crossed the house and ascended his own flight up to his private quarters.

There were times when a guy just had to be alone.

She should have kept her mouth shut. Just because she saw something as healing didn't mean that others would. Or that they were in a mental state to be healed. Watching Weston fingering his boyhood sheets, seeing the longing on his face, she'd wanted to help. To ease his suffering.

Instead, she'd pissed him off.

Taking sheets from the linen closet, Paige made her bed. And then started the onerous process of hauling all of her earthly belongings from the downstairs bedroom, and the garage, up to her new quarters. The clothes were always the worst, but she had a system, hauling filled hangers in groups of twenty, saving lightest for last.

She'd peeked into the room next door to hers after Weston's abrupt departure, and, thrilled to see a desk and bookshelves there, in addition to a twin bed, she claimed the room as an office-cum-sitting room. But didn't want to move in until he'd had a chance to check out the space as well.

Figuring she had enough to keep her busy until this evening's feeding time, she worked on getting moved into the bedroom portion of her new home, taking a time-out every hour or so to visit the dogs. They'd done pretty well with Walter's absence, except for Buddy peeing on the floor more, and Checkers sleeping more, but she'd been spending extra time with them every day since then as well and wasn't going to stop.

Especially not with someone new in their midst.

Her phone rang toward the end of the afternoon, startling her so much she dropped the razor she'd been about to place on the lower built-in shower shelf.

It wasn't that she didn't ever get phone calls—she did, quite often, with friends checking in from various places she'd lived, visited or worked at one time or another—she'd just been so deep in thought about her housemate that she'd been startled back to real time.

It bothered her that Weston was on the phone and the subject of her thoughts. As though she'd conjured him. She knew people who believed in such possibilities. And while the idea of it was kind of cool, she was still on the fence with the reality of it.

But if it really happened…she didn't want to have that kind of soul connection with her reluctant housemate.

"Hello?" They'd exchanged cell numbers the first day they'd met. Neither of them had ever used them to contact the other before.

"I apologize for my abrupt departure. It was rude."

"Are you kidding? You were upset and wanted to be alone with your feelings. You have no reason to apologize for that. I'll try to be more circumspect in the future when sharing what I know." They weren't going to make it a year if they had to tiptoe around and apologize every time one or the other of them burped.

It happened.

"You raise your voice to me, start acting mean, or eat all the bread without telling me it's gone, then you'd need to apologize." She picked up the razor. Put it in place.

"I was calling to suggest that we lay some ground rules for our behavior over the next year. I guess you've just put the first one on the list."

Standing in the door between her bathroom, so large it was like a suite unto itself, and bedroom, she paused, asking, "Wouldn't it be easier to make the list if we were sitting together with the computer right there to take down the notes?"

"One of my ground rules has to be in place before we're together again."

Of course it did. With a small smile on her face, she sat on the side of the bed, looking out the French doors to the balcony. She needed outdoor furniture.

Before another night passed.

How cool would it be to sit out there at night before bed and just chill?

"Give it to me," she told the prickly man on the other end of the line. Not really liking her mental description of Walter's son. He was definitely prickly on the surface, but she was beginning to suspect that those sharp edges didn't even get to skin-deep. And they weren't there to hurt others. They were there to help him protect himself.

Not that any of that was any of her business. Or concern.

She wasn't even interested. Just noting what was right in front of her. Like the fact that the sun was shining.

"No more personal talk unless the one it concerns brings it up."

Uh-huh. Well, she'd been told to mind her own business. But he'd done it politely. With kindness. No reason her feelings should be hurt.

They weren't really. Her ego was just bruised a bit.

She'd been trying to gift him with insights from his father.

"So, just to clarify, when we're going through rooms, if I know of a story about particular furnishings or possessions, should I not share them?"

"Those you can share."

"But if I know why Walter bought it, I shouldn't share that."

"You can share that, too. Anything personal to my father, you can share. I want to know."

Her ruffled feathers smoothing out nicely, she nodded, and might even have preened and grinned, if he'd have been there to see it. Just why the grin would be for him, she didn't want to ask herself. She didn't want the answer. But said, "Okay, so I'm not supposed to ask about, or talk about, you, and you'll do the same with me, unless we bring up a topic ourselves."

"Yes. That."

"You got a computer there? Jotting this down? That's two rules, so far. Or maybe four if we take mine for three separate ones. Do we organize it by apology? If so, it's just one. But if we're going to go for bread as a stand-in for all kitchen food, then maybe we should list separately." She kept her tone even.

"I think we're understanding each other enough to do without a written list."

She thought so, too, and agreed to meet him at the end of the hall to continue with their perusal of the rooms on her wing.

He'd reached out. They'd resolved the tension between them.

And she felt a little like singing as she hung up the phone.

Weston had changed into jeans, a T-shirt and tennis shoes, figuring he might need to move some furniture or some other such things. He had the one day and then had to get back to building his business, and then would do what he could at home in the evenings.

Paige would need to work as well. He had no idea about any other jobs she had going, but knew that the deadline for his father's memoirs was rapidly approaching and she'd said she still had three chapters to write.

On Tuesday he planned to find office space,

and then put out feelers for a receptionist/secretary familiar with the accounting field. His new client transitioned from another firm in another few weeks and he wanted everything running smoothly by the time that happened.

In the meantime, he'd held on to a few of his biggest accounts in Ohio, small businesses in his hometown who'd wanted to stay with him in spite of his move. They were people who were loyal to him.

People he was loyal to.

He'd need to keep up with their daily accountings.

And he liked Paige's idea of turning the bedroom down the hall from her into her study, thinking of a room he'd passed by on his own hallway that could serve a similar purpose for him. Once she'd been through it, of course.

"There's an office downstairs," Paige told him when he divulged his plan as they stood in her chosen study room together. "Your father used it regularly. I figured you would, too."

"Maybe someday in the future. For now, I'll use the room upstairs."

"While I'm here," she said, nodding.

The woman's inability to keep potentially uncomfortable comments to herself, to instead just throw them out into their shared air, was both edifying and disruptive.

He knew where he stood with her. There'd be no

hidden minefields in their midst. But she made it difficult for them to remain as distant as he'd determined they would be.

Difficult, but not impossible.

Just as she could set her own comfort level in terms of the words that came out of her mouth, so could he, in his lack of engaging with them. Or his lack of speaking his own.

She hadn't changed from the high-waisted magenta-and-white shirt she'd had on that morning. And earlier in the afternoon. For a second there, when he glanced at her, he had a flash of the tender flesh underneath that skirt—a very distinct memory that kept repeating itself.

"And back to our nonwritten list of rules of engagement…" As before, she didn't take a hint from his silence, but rather, took it as an invitation to keep talking. In this case, the distraction was more welcome than the avenue his thoughts had traveled down. He listened more eagerly as she continued, "I have another topic that we need to hash out in a way that satisfies us both."

She'd mentioned, when they'd first entered the room, that the only thing she'd like better about her new study was if there was a couch along the far wall instead of the twin bed. He pulled the comforter off the bed, intending to dismantle it and get it out of her way. "Shoot," he said, reaching for the top mattress, picking it up and carrying it toward the door.

"Guests," she said.

Balancing the mattress top up along the wall outside the door, he went back for the box springs. "Guess?" he repeated. "You want me to guess your topic?"

Was she kidding?

A quick glance at those dark blue eyes and youthful, open features, told him she was serious.

"Guests," she repeated, with exaggerated enunciation. "Guests. As in, people who come to stay with us."

There was no *us*. Setting down the box spring with its counterpart, he entered the room ready to tell her so. He had to lay down the law immediately. Start out as he meant to go on.

No other way they'd last a year...

"Us individually," she clarified after one look at his face. What now? She was reading his mind like a tarot reader?

"I don't plan to have any guests," he told her. That one was simple.

"So *my* guests," she clarified yet again. And she wasn't budging. Arms crossed, she stood in front of the bed frame, as though guarding it. Preventing him from avoiding paying full attention to the conversation by keeping busy, apparently.

At least that was how he took it.

A few feet away from her, he stopped. Folding his own arms, and said, "I don't have any rules for your guests," he said. If they were male, all the better.

He could quit picturing her thighs like they came with the house. Like they could share them, too, as they were sharing everything else on the estate.

"I do have rules."

Her tone of voice…her stance…it was so… determined. Curiously lacking any of her usual openness.

Her position definitely read as, "No welcome here." So maybe the guests were female. And he wasn't supposed to hit on them? No problem. As if he would ever do such a thing.

"You think I'm going to impose myself on your guests?"

"No, I think they're going to do everything in their power to impose themselves on you, and I won't have it."

Maybe she needed to rethink her guest list.

"It sounds like your ground rules might need to be for them."

"Believe me, if I could find a way to get my… guests… to abide by them, I'd have them set in gold and hand the regulations to them on a silver platter."

Exasperation, frustration and…something else laced her tone. The something else was what caught his attention.

"Here's a suggestion…don't invite them here."

Whoever "they" were, she seemed honestly bothered by what they might do.

Was she afraid they'd rob the place?

And the damned rule wasn't working. How could they talk if they couldn't ask personal questions? She wasn't telling him who was coming, and he couldn't ask, but he was supposed to engage in conversation about their visit?

"If only it were that simple. As soon as I give them my new address, they're going to be knocking on the door. Give or take the day or two it will take them to make arrangements at work and get here from Michigan."

"Don't give them your address then." The answer was so simple. And he found it fascinating that she hadn't already resolved not to do so. She'd seemed so determined in his dealings with her, so in charge—with the dogs, with following Walter's wishes—the scene unfolding before him didn't make sense.

"If only. The second they find out I'm not at my old address, they'll contact the police and file a missing person's report."

"Not if you're in touch with them. Text, phone…"

"They'll be certain that someone is sending false texts or making me say whatever has to be said." She was shaking her head, as though acknowledging the unusual circumstances of it all, but her frown was dead serious.

When he realized that he was getting sucked in, that he cared way too much about that frown, about her distress, he said, "So give me whatever boundaries you've worked out for guests."

It's what he should have led with. He'd be more careful in the future.

"When we have guests, they are not free to roam the mansion. They have to stay only in the kitchen, the kennel and our own separate wings of the upstairs. And we are to respect those areas we both normally inhabit when guests are present and not enter the occupied space." She looked away as she said that last bit.

"When you have guests, I'm to stay out of the kitchen and the kennel?"

"Only when the guests are present in those rooms."

The kitchen...he didn't give two hoots about that. He'd already pretty much determined he wouldn't be using it. Just couldn't see himself sharing a refrigerator with this woman and remaining detached.

Stupid, maybe, but in his mind, food always brought people together. That's why friends met for meals. And why it mattered that families sat down together for dinner at night. Even if dinner was only a bowl of canned soup night after night.

But the kennel...

"I can give you the kitchen as a free zone, but not the kennel," he said.

Her nod came quickly, as though she'd been expecting the response. "We can work out some kind of communication between the two of us. You let me know when you want to be in the kennel and I'll make sure they aren't there."

"I want feeding times."

Her eyes closed, her chin scrunched up a bit and then, with an expression so sad he almost changed his mind, she nodded. "Fine. You get all feeding times when I have guests." And then, looking more like herself, she added, "But other than that, you give me space in the kennel, and I'll let you know when it's free in case you want to visit the dogs."

She'd capitulated far too easily, making him more curious about the situation than ever. Her guests were apparently coming, whether she wanted them or not. And she very badly didn't want them anywhere near him.

His interest in her grew some more.

"You can have one feeding a day and I'll take the other. But I get Checkers at night," he amended.

The smile that concession earned him almost made him hard.

She stepped away from the remainder of the bed, allowing him access, seeming to indicate that the conversation was over.

For once, he was the one who wasn't done.

He had to know more.

Who were her guests? How could she be so sure

they'd be coming? And why did they have such weird power over her?

Why wasn't she spilling words all over him?

He watched her run her fingers over the bookcase. Look in the desk drawer.

The conversation was over. For now, anyway. He knew he'd want to find out exactly who these people were that would be staying in his home. *Their* home?

And as much as he wanted to know more, because he did, he would not ask another question. He went to work on the bed frame, knowing that his decision to let his curiosity go was not only for the best overall, but would be the only way to get them through the year ahead, together.

Chapter Ten

They'd found a couch in another room along her hallway that fit her new study perfectly, right down to the mauve color and clawed feet. And between the two of them, they managed to lift it and get it in through the doorway.

They ordered pizza to share, agreeing on a barbecue chicken specialty, and then stood in the kennel eating it, while the dogs munched down their own dinners.

"The twin bed would look good over on that wall," West said in between bites, pointing to the empty space just to the left of the door leading out from the laundry room. "We could keep a cover on it for the dogs' use, and if there was ever occasion for either one of us to be out here overnight, you know, watching over a sick pup, the bed would be a hell of a lot more comfortable than either of those couches."

He was looking around the room as he took another bite, his hip leaning against the counter. For a second there, listening to him, seeing the interested expression on his very handsome face, looking at that body, Paige wanted him to be her man.

Not permanently or anything. But for a moment or two.

She'd had men in her life. One, Lonnie, for over six months.

A year would be too long. Six months had been too long. Things had gotten a little messy when she'd had to get out. She'd hurt a great man, and had been hurt as well…

"You don't agree? You think the bed's a bad idea?"

"No! I don't think it's a bad idea. I think it's a great idea," she said, filling her mouth with a big bite of pizza before she rambled on to fill the silence.

West didn't need to know details about her past failed relationships.

And she most certainly wasn't about to reveal her current yearnings for him.

They ate in silence for a minute or two. Darcy, Abe and Erin, the fastest eaters, had appeared at their feet, begging for droppings. The others would be over soon, maybe even Annie, who liked chicken sometimes.

"The vet says we should stay away from feeding the rescues table food, except for boiled chicken and rice sometimes to induce weight gain. Keeping them on their own diets is not only good for their overall health and weight maintenance, but it also prevents failed expectations as they're adopted and move to new homes. A regime of no table food also helps discourage the bad behavior of begging. Once in their new homes, it's up to the new owners whether or not they want to treat them to table food at their discretion." She was rambling and didn't care. At least she wasn't fully focused on kissing those lips that were just a tad bit shiny, moist from the tongue that had just licked crumbs off them.

"Walter didn't agree," she continued, barely taking a breath, as she forced her gaze to stay pointed at the canine companions. "He said they'd already had tough lives and a little spoiling would help them to warm up and trust people. Anytime he snacked in here, he shared with them."

With that, she shoved a piece of crust in her mouth instead of dropping it to the floor. And reached for the box of dog treats in the cupboard right above them, dispersing them to everyone equally. Even Annie, who took hers over to a canine bed, dropped it and lay down on top of it.

"Okay, who are these guests of yours?" To say she was startled by the blurted question was an understatement. With her hand suspended over the next piece of pizza she'd had her eye on, Paige pulled her arm back, fingers empty.

"I've given it some thought, and while we are co-owners, and both responsible for the estate, we should at least know the identities of anyone staying on the premises."

His argument made good sense. Of course.

And there she'd been, feeling all good about the fact that he hadn't bothered to ask about her visitors earlier. She'd thought she was off the hook.

"This doesn't in any way negate the previously agreed-upon boundaries pertaining to guests once they're here," he said, as though trying to reassure her.

"Yes, but we have the boundary of no personal conversation that isn't introduced by the one it's personal to."

Her life was her business, period. Purposely preserved just as it was. Perfect for her.

Walter didn't even know the details she could see Weston eventually requesting.

"Right." He nodded slowly, still eating.

She'd lost her appetite.

"But this isn't just personal as it pertains to occupants of our joint property. If the visitor were a celebrity, for instance, and her presence here became known, it could make life difficult for both owners, not just the one who'd invited the famous guest."

Lord help her, was she going to make it a week with West Thomas? Let alone a year?

Movement off to the left caught her peripheral vision, and she glanced over in time to see Annie stand up in the round cushioned bed, take the treat in her mouth and eat it.

The little dog's victory reminded her who she was. Why she was there. And it had nothing to do with her own small comforts.

Or discomforts, either.

She'd survived much worse than a year with Weston Thomas would be, no matter what hell it turned into.

"My only visitors will be my sisters," she told him, doing her best to keep her voice even. Nonchalant.

"Your sisters?" She felt the interest in his glance even without looking at him directly. She heard it in his tone, too.

"Yes. My sisters." Smart man that he was, he'd better pick up quickly on her tone, too. She'd answered his question and they were done.

"How many are there?"

The additional question was fair. "Two."

"The siblings for whom you're on social media."

She'd forgotten she'd mentioned that. "One account only, on the most private settings…" Lest he try again to find anything about her that way. He wouldn't be successful. "And, yes, those are them."

"How would they know that you aren't at your previous physical address? You said they'd file a missing person's report if you weren't there."

Right. And their "no personal conversation" boundary didn't apply to the question because she was the one who'd offered the information to begin with.

The whole "having guests" portion of the conversation had started with her, too.

She was going to have to rethink the rules. Find some that suited her better.

Or learn to keep her mouth shut around him.

She was so good at keeping to herself, in general. Why did her mouth have the runs around him?

"Your silence makes me wonder if I need to be worried here."

He was still chomping away, though.

Mixed with the current conversation, the smell of the pizza was making her slightly nauseous.

"They send me things. Little stuff just to say I love you. They get delivery reports and if I don't respond the same day, they call the police."

There. It was out. He might have discovered something to that effect eventually, anyway, because she was going to have to be anal about getting any packages left for her on the day they were left. He couldn't, say, take delivery at the door and leave the package, say, in the kennel one evening, for her to find the next day.

He'd stopped eating. Was staring at her. Put down the remainder of his food. She could feel the questions coming.

Knew she'd been the one to bring them on herself.

She'd opened the door to them.

Still didn't make her ready to stand there and answer them.

Excusing herself, Paige left the room.

She'd done it again. This whole walking-out-on-him thing had to stop.

He'd bring forth another rule to that effect.

And there was no better time than the present.

Closing up the pizza box, putting it in the refrigerator, he patted each dog on the head, uttered some kind words and went in search of his co-owner.

He found her upstairs in her study room, sitting on the newly moved mauve couch, unpacking a box. Her skirt hung safely to the floor.

Technically, he wasn't supposed to be there as they'd finished going through the rooms on that hallway, making it officially hers and off-limits to him unless he was invited.

"I just came up to get the bed," he improvised, but he was telling the truth, too. If not for the furniture, he wouldn't have ventured into her space without invitation. And she'd have heard him coming. Could have told him to go away.

Boundaries were boundaries.

"But this habit of yours of walking out…it's not conducive to a good business relationship."

Pulling the small box of paper-wrapped items up to her chest, she rested her arms on it, and nodded. "I know. You're right. And I apologize."

Well, then. Good.

Still, he stood there in the doorway, nodding, looking at her. "It's just… I wasn't meaning to pry down there. It's just, this stuff with your sisters, it's all a bit…unusual…and since we share this property…if police are going to be showing up looking for you, I feel that I have a right to a heads-up as to why."

The point was completely, 100 percent valid. He wanted that to be the only reason he was asking.

And knew it wasn't. If she was in some kind of trouble, or danger, he just had to know.

At her continued silence, he said, "Tell me about them, at least. You said they're from Michigan. Do they live in the same place?"

"Why is that pertinent?" She hugged her box like a shield. He wanted her to know she had nothing to fear from him. He was a small-town accountant who liked both feet on the ground.

"It's not."

And why was something that innocuous so much of an issue for her that she hadn't answered?

"Yes, they live in the same town." And then, grudgingly, she added, "Next door to each other."

That was close. And not something you heard a lot. Just the idea of two houses side by side being for sale at the same time…maybe even in the same decade…

"Are they older than you? Younger? One of each?"

"Older."

Okay, so that could explain why they watched over her. Just not to the extent of calling the police when she didn't respond to a package. Or thinking someone else would be answering a text or forcing her to answer her phone…

"How much older?"

"Four years."

"And?" he asked, when she didn't offer the second sibling's age.

"That's it. Four years."

Only one way that happened, assuming they were biological siblings. "They're twins?"

"Yes."

"Are they cops or something? Federal agents? Do they fear they're bringing harm down on you? Or have reason to think someone is going to go after you to retaliate against them?" So, yeah, maybe he watched a little too much crime television.

When you lived in a town where the only thing to do past five was hang out in one of the local bars, you either drank too much or found other things to do. But she was definitely hiding something, which gave him true cause to be uneasy.

And to be worried for her.

"Mariah manages a team of home health care workers and Tess is a librarian."

Not much cause for calling police inherent there.

"And, okay." Setting aside her box, she stood up.

"This is all getting much bigger than it needed to be. Our parents died young, in a van mishap. The girls were fifteen at the time and took me under their wing. They're way too overprotective, and I humor that because I love them dearly, and I understand how the…accident…affected them. I swear to you—" she stepped closer, meeting his gaze head-on as she imparted those four words "—there is no danger, past or present, waiting to befall me. My sisters did everything they could to keep me close, but I'm not like them. I have my own set of boundaries, ones that let me fly. I live the life I need to live, not the life they'd like me to live. I don't stay in one place. And I don't fear what bad things might happen. I'm not going to spend my life looking over my shoulder. Unless it's to smile at a memory."

He believed every word. And his heart ached for her. Because what she wasn't saying was that she'd been eleven when her parents had died.

That couldn't have been easy.

He understood her wanting to keep that pain private.

"They're afraid of losing you, too," he said aloud.

"Yes."

"How soon can I expect them to show up on our doorstep?" How long was she going to put off telling them she'd moved?

"Their flight lands Wednesday afternoon."

"As in two days from now?" he asked, surprised. And yet, not as completely as he might have been.

"Yes."

She'd obviously made the call that afternoon, after their talk about guests. Things were becoming a little clearer. The imminent call she had to make had prompted the whole visitor conversation. Which gave him a little more insight into the mysteries that made up her whole being. She didn't give in to her loved ones' desires for her life, but she seemed to respect their position enough to tend to their fears where she was concerned.

Personally, he thought them way overboard in their protectiveness, to the point of maybe needing to see someone about it, but hc wasn't there to judge.

Or to find her patience with, and care for, her older sisters rather sweet.

He was just her temporary business partner.

Certainly not a protector or lover.

Not even a friend.

And mostly, he wanted to be good with that.

"You want the night feeding then, so you can introduce them to the dogs?"

"Yes, thank you, that would be great." The effects of her slow smile landed somewhere within his chest, slid down to his gut and lingered.

Forecasting a problem he was choosing to ignore.

Chapter Eleven

At Paige's instigation, they worked for another couple hours Monday night. They reviewed the laundry area after they got the bed set up, with only a dog-friendly coverlet on top of the mattress, in the kennel.

It had taken them no time to finish her hallway earlier. They'd all been furniture only, just like the first room they'd seen had been. It didn't take her long to realize she'd chosen the wing of the house that Walter had barely occupied. She now knew the previous owner had only used the space as guest rooms and hadn't had any affinity for the furnishings.

It seemed fitting to her that she'd been drawn to the nonpermanent, nonfamilial area. Not that she told West so.

"Some people think that I'm a runner," she confided in him as they moved from downstairs space to his wing, skipping the upstairs wing that connected hers and his for the time being. She'd suggested that they take the rest of Monday night, and whatever time he had on Tuesday, to at least get through their two hallways so that they were each free to do whatever they wanted within their own space.

So that they each had their own separate areas.

The first room they'd entered had contained two floor-to-ceiling completely filled built-in bookcases. She was going through one wall, pulling out anything she'd want; he was doing the same with the other, and then they'd switch. When they were done, they'd go through each other's choices and make decisions on a book-by-book basis.

"If you're referring to what happened downstairs at dinner, don't worry about it," he told her, standing on a rolling ladder attached to ceiling runners. He was still on his first shelf of books and had already amassed an impressive pile of wants.

She was just a quarter of the way through her own first shelf, also atop a matching ladder, but her keep pile only had one item. Unlike the man who would spend the rest of his life in a huge house, she traveled light.

Which meant she had to negotiate access to the rest of the books she'd be wanting to read in the 361 days she had left. By the size of his stack, she figured she could probably trade her access for his ownership if she played her cards right.

Since she'd once ghostwritten a massive biography for a former card sharp, she figured the odds were fairly well in her favor.

"I was just letting you know that you aren't alone in your assessment," she told him, feeling so much more relaxed, and a whole lot more like herself, now that her sisters were dealt with.

First, she'd called them, and they'd taken the news of her move better than she'd expected. And second, their visit would be separate and removed from interaction with West Thomas. Yay!

"As long as we're good with our understanding in that regard, we're done there," he said a bit distractedly, his full attention seeming to be on the page he was perusing.

Still, accidents happened, and what if Mariah or Tess stumbled upon him...and started talking?

"I just want you to know that I don't ever run out on sealed deals, or break my word when I say I'm going to do something."

Tess, more than Mariah, might warn him that even her grandparents had been concerned about her constant need to get up and go. Her refusal to stay in any one place for more than a year or two—she'd had to attend three different universities to even get her degree.

That they all, even her ex, Lonnie, and maybe even Walter, were worried sick about her as the years passed and she didn't grow out of her penchant for running away.

"Paige?"

Turning on her ladder, she saw West sitting on

the top step of his, his hands free of books as he watched her.

"Yeah?"

"Why would you think you'd need to warn me about something like that?"

She shrugged, turned back to the shelf she'd been staring at but not touching. "With my sisters coming and all…if our plan fails and they find you alone… there's no telling what they might say."

Not about the carjacking. No one mentioned that. Not after the debilitating hounding of well-wishers, benefactors, sympathy offerers and curiosity mongers in the months and then years that followed. Everyone had thought at first that she'd been kidnapped and her face had been plastered all over every major and a lot of minor news sources in the country. After she'd been found, unharmed, that photo had circulated again and that same photo, along with her and her sisters' names, kept coming up again and again. There'd been the trial. She'd testified behind a one-way mirror but some less reputable news sources had used the stock photo.

The man's death in prison. Her picture again, her sisters' names.

Finally, at the advice of a lawyer, their grandparents had had their names changed from Anders to their mother's maiden name, Martinson, so that the girls, and young Paige in particular, could get some peace.

"Just so you know…" West's voice brought her up out of hell and back to him. Just as she'd been brought back by others over and over during the first months after she'd returned home. And then by associates throughout the years. However, warmth flooding her with her snap back to the moment, was new.

As was the even tide of consciousness that accompanied her return. There was no emotional lurch. No need to gather herself; she was already busy following the rest of his sentence.

"…I don't form my opinions of a person based on what others have to say about them. Not even older sisters. Especially not older sisters, whose opinion couldn't help but be biased by their close association."

She nodded, feeling better than she had in a while.

"I don't base them on my father's opinions, either," he added. He was still looking at her and she had a feeling she was supposed to be getting something.

"I'm choosing to trust you because I find myself unable not to do so."

Oh. Deflation hit with a thud. "Because the will gives you no other choice." Not even Walter's opinion was going to sway him.

"No, because I believe you, even though I've thought about all of the possible reasons for not doing so."

Oh! Okay. She grinned. "You trust me."

"I do."

"Well, for what it's worth, I trust you, too."

The room got thick then, and warning bells went off loud and clear inside her. So she quickly added, "And my trust is only partially because of all the stories Walter told me about you as a kid." The rest was because of Weston himself.

He'd given her absolute trust.

She'd given him what she had…trust from a distance.

With one foot out the door.

Weston worked on Tuesday, meeting with a Realtor to look at the office space he'd already scouted out before his father's death. He wanted to own, not rent, and could afford to buy a nice suite in a high-rise building only ten miles up the highway.

He could have put the appointment off a day or two, could have done it all after Paige's sisters were in town, and probably, assuming the offer he'd made was accepted, would meet with other owners in the building and with a contractor to firm up plans, just to keep himself off the Walter Thomas premises.

But after four days of nothing but Paige, he had to get out into the world. The woman was starting to affect him. Like she was putting a spell on him or something.

The last thought was ludicrous. He knew that.

Hadn't lost his faculties to that extent. But the way he was drawn to her, the depth of his heartbreak for the eleven-year-old child who'd lost her parents in a van accident, and his admiration for the strength of the woman who stood up to her older sisters for her own autonomy and yet still had the compassion to tend to them… If he didn't know better, he'd think he was starting to really care about her.

After just four days.

Yeah, right.

More like his father's death was affecting him far more intensely than he'd at first thought.

He was fine. And he'd be fine.

But his heart had a serious crack in it.

He had to let it heal. Not try to fill in the gap with his housemate's mysterious aura.

So thinking, he was armed with emotional barriers and a conversation plan when he met Paige in the kennel on Tuesday evening. They planned to have leftover pizza and feed the dogs before heading back upstairs to the library room they'd only half finished. Whatever didn't get done on his hallway that night would have to wait until after her sisters' departure on Sunday. He'd prefer to have it all done.

To know that Paige wouldn't be back on those floorboards ever again.

The sooner that happened, the better for all parts of him.

Their time in the kennel was spent completely

focused on the dogs. She told him what Annie had eaten that day—not enough—and that Buddy had peed outside every time.

And that Checkers had pooped on the pad twice.

"I think he missed you," she said.

Weston didn't think so, but the idea didn't displease him, either. "I'll take him with me tomorrow," he told her. His offer on the suite had already been accepted. And the building allowed animals. It was something he'd verified only that morning. Not anything he'd have thought to care about when he'd first been to the property, and yet something that had sealed the deal as far as he was concerned. "There's a nice dog park in the quad of the building. I'll take pads, too," he offered to the room in general.

"You've already got space?"

"The deal hasn't closed yet, of course, but my offer was accepted, and the seller has agreed to allow me in immediately. I'll be responsible for any build-out expense and will lose anything I spend if the deal doesn't close as expected. But as a negotiated incentive, I only have to pay ten dollars in rent for early occupancy."

She asked pertinent questions about the suite, the square footage, how he wanted to break it out, and when he barely managed to stop himself from inviting her to visit, to ask for any input she had to offer, he immediately mandated to himself that conversation pertaining to his new office was off-limits.

Then he escaped outside to spend a few minutes with the animals before heading back upstairs. She'd been with them on and off all day and had said she'd clean up the small dinner mess. She was also stopping off in the kitchen to make tea and had offered to fix some coffee for him.

Even that seemed too intimate to him at that moment, so he'd declined. And grabbed a bottle of water out of the refrigerator in the kennel to take upstairs with him. He'd already changed out his business attire for jeans and another T-shirt before dinner and so headed straight to the library. They needed to move quickly if they were going to get her permanently done with that hallway before morning.

Paige, in colorful leggings, a midthigh-length pink-and-purple shirt and pink studded flip-flops, was already there before him, and up on her ladder. While he liked the idea of her legs encased in fabric that could not give him inadvertent glances of private flesh, he had to swallow twice at the sight of that backside perched so deliciously on the board.

In the kennel, with both of them standing, her long flowing shirt had completely hidden those particular assets from him.

Turning his back as his body started to respond to her, he climbed his ladder and forced himself to read words on pages. As many times as it took to distract his focus from that which he could not have.

West seemed edgy. Which made Paige edgy.

Her sisters' imminent plundering of her space didn't help matters. So when he started talking about finances, she was only too happy to engage in the conversation.

And agreed with everything he laid out in terms of managing the estate. They'd have bimonthly meetings to discuss expenses and pay bills.

They'd each be responsible for their own personal expenditures, but the estate would buy paper products, trash bags, laundry supplies and the like.

"Walter had a cleaning service come in twice a week," she told him, not sure how much he knew. Since he was his father's accountant, she figured it was pretty much everything.

"I was thinking we'd continue with that practice," he told her. "And I meant to ask, do we need to call them to resume service? Weren't they due here today?"

"They were. Tuesdays and Fridays. You slept through Friday's visit and they were here today."

"They left a bill?"

"I paid them. Your dad had a card on file, but I didn't feel comfortable using that as I don't know if it was his personal card, or in the name of the estate."

He turned on the ladder just as she glanced over in his direction and for a second there, they just looked at each other. It was the weirdest thing.

Then he said, "I'll reimburse you first thing tomorrow."

"Don't worry about it, West. I'm not going to do well here if we nickel-and-dime every little thing."

"But you shouldn't be out for cleaning this place. I've seen the bill. It isn't cheap."

"I can afford it." It was best he know that. She wasn't rich to Walter's standards, but neither was she some pauper, living off a good thing that had come her way.

He was still looking at her—studying her was more like it—so she turned back to the shelf she'd been mentally cataloguing. Travel books. From many places she might like to go.

"This isn't the first time you've paid an expense for the estate, is it?"

There'd been the landscaper once, when Walter's card had expired and he'd been in town having lunch with a friend. And a plumber he'd had her call once when he'd been off fishing for the weekend. She shrugged.

"Seriously, Paige. That's not right. My father, he's never had a good head for financial matters, and it's wrong that you'd have to pay for that. Wrong of him not to have been more aware."

The genuine anger in his tone had her turning

back around. His frown looked fiercer than she'd seen it to date. "Seriously, West," she mimicked him. "It's not a big deal."

"It is to me."

"I'm getting that. What, you don't like that you might be indebted to someone for something?"

He shook his head. Took out a book, opened it, while she continued to watch him. Trying to figure him out.

When he looked back over at her, he seemed, more weary than anything. "Growing up, my dad… he'd get so into whatever invention he was working on—so excited about how much it was going to earn us—as soon as he'd acquired a patent on the next great idea, he'd spend money for the electric bill or groceries on parts or supplies. We were down to the thirty-days-late mark on the mortgage more often than not, too. And the ideas…they were so out there. A magnetic belt that would hold all your gadgets, except that, with magnets, things tend to fall off when bumped, your gadgets would need some kind of magnetic attachment, and the polarizing forces were an issue, too."

She chuckled and he stared at her. "I'm sorry. I was just remembering him telling me how he'd taught you all about polarization and how you had to have a north and south pole in order for the magnetic forces to be attracted to each other. You were seven at the time. And you somehow rigged the gadgets he was using to test his belt so that when he went to wear them, they'd all repel and fall off."

His smile was slow in coming, but it got there. "I'd actually forgotten about that," he said. And then chuckled, too.

"And the hand grip that was supposed to get bags off the carousel at the airport."

"He insisted we go the airport on Sunday evening, when the place was packed with weekenders coming home, and he was going to show me how his hand grip would impress the ladies. Instead, the grip got caught in a latch and he spilled a woman's lingerie on the floor..."

She laughed out loud, remembering Walter's rendition of the story. He'd been a very colorful storyteller.

A colorful man.

She'd envied West, getting to grow up with any father, let alone one who was so fun.

"His words to me were, 'Why couldn't it have been books? Or shoes?'"

"It was just a little case. He was starting out small."

And the project had failed because there had been no way to quickly attach the grip to the case. Walter had told her that, too.

"The most expensive had been the grocery cart return," he said, frowning again. "He'd scaled down the model, of course, but there was supposed to be a track that was installed underground, with an entrance point in the parking lot, and an exit up in front of the store, that would feed carts out already joined in a line. The theory was kind of like a bowling ball return system. He was certain when he got that patent that our ship was coming in. He borrowed the money on a six-month, short-term loan, and we ended up losing our house. Had to sell it for the equity and move into a smaller place."

"He said you liked the place better because it was closer to school and you didn't have to ride with him every day. And that your room was actually bigger."

Walter had been a high school science teacher by trade and in the small town where West had grown up, every kid in town either had had, or would have, his dad for a teacher at some point. She'd found the idea comforting. Had tried to imagine how cool that would be.

"It was old, run-down and the roof leaked," he said. "Though I did like being able to make my own way to school. And my room, with a built-in desk and extra outlets everywhere, turned out to be a techie's dream." He was smiling again. And then sobered.

"My father is the reason I became an accountant. The first year we were in that house, the electricity was turned off twice. By the time I was in high school, I ended up taking over the household finances. I just couldn't live like that anymore, worrying I'd go in to shower some morning and have no water."

Walter hadn't mentioned anything about the electricity. The water. She guessed because all that hadn't mattered to him, but she could see how it would matter to a young West. Could see how hard it had been, growing up as he had. Hearing another side of the story gave her a whole new insight into the son Walter had raised. A man she was beginning to like more than a little bit.

Gave her an understanding she maybe didn't need.

Since they were just co-owners of an estate. Not even roommates, really. More like living in separate condos with one roof. And some shared facilities.

But at least she wasn't fretting about her sisters descending upon her the following afternoon.

Instead, she was noticing how much she liked the warm glow in West's eyes as his gaze held hers for a second time.

That probably wasn't a good thing, either.

Chapter Twelve

He wanted her. Plain and simple. Nothing else attached. This woman was so different from any he'd ever known. Maybe it was that she knew his father so well. That she knew Weston, was privy to his stories before he even told them.

Maybe she was just so good at what she did for a living that she could draw a story out of anyone.

He had a lot of maybes, no answers and one very definite, unrelated conclusion.

He absolutely could not, ever, act upon his desire. You couldn't always help what you felt, but you could damn sure help what you did with it. Or about it.

Sitting there, holding her gaze, he didn't want to look away. Didn't want her to, either. And knew he had to do something to break the contact before it was too late.

"Dogs," he said. Shook his head. And started again. "I wanted to talk to you about another financial expenditure."

She turned back to her books. "Sure, what's up?"

The preplanned conversational starter had served

its purpose. Now he had to actually have the conversation.

"I'd like to build a second kennel, like you mentioned the other day."

"I didn't mention it. You did. You wanted me to build one on another property."

"And you said we could do it here and I think you're right."

"You're taking my words out of context. I was only responding to what you'd said."

Was she being purposely difficult? Could he blame her if she was?

"Are you opposed to it? We could take in double the rescues while still maintaining a sense of home for them."

"With the same pen? Or different ones? It might be a lot of dogs in one space."

"That's what I was thinking. But there's that little morning space off the piano room on the other side of the living area. We could build over there. And take turns with feedings and things. I'd do one kennel in the morning and the other at night and you could do the same. That way the dogs would still get both of us every day."

"And we could both do both sometimes, so they get used to having more than one person around at a time."

His idea had involved not seeing her every day,

but she made a good point. Some days they could both do both.

"The main thing is that we could take in more dogs."

"Agreed. But…what about when I go? That'll be an awful lot for you to deal with."

He put a couple of books in his keep pile, currently sitting on the edge of the shelf below the one where he was working. "I'm a single guy living alone. I can handle two kennels on my own. And I work from home some days, too, and the dogs can take turns coming to work with me. I can also hire someone at that point to come in during the day."

He wanted the second kennel. Would have it even if he had to wait the year. The project…one of his father's ideas that worked, actually, appealed to him in ways he hadn't imagined.

Gave him a sense of family he hadn't known he'd been missing.

"Sounds like you've given this serious thought."

"I have."

"Then let's do it. I can contact the people Walter used to build the first room and pen."

"And have them expand the current pen, too," he suggested.

"I'll call them in the morning."

He glanced at her just as she turned her face toward him. She was smiling.

And he smiled, too.

"Hey, about earlier…it was nice, the way you reminded me of aspects of things that I'd forgotten. The magnetic belt trick I'd played, I haven't thought of that in years. And having a bigger room… Anyway, thank you."

"No problem!" She climbed down her ladder with only one book in hand again. That made two for her keep pile. "I'm really glad to share whatever I can," she said easily.

Too easily?

"Paige?" He climbed down, too. Took a step toward her and stopped.

"You've done more than share. You've given me back something I didn't even know I'd lost. And shown me a side of myself I'm not all that fond of, too. I was so busy seeing what my dad didn't do that I didn't appreciate enough all the great things he did. He wasn't perfect, but he was there."

She froze, her gaze locked with his once again. Something about those magnetic poles, maybe. "I'm sorry yours couldn't be there for you."

Pulling in her lower lip, she nodded. Blinked a time or two. And then smiled at him.

But up close, he noticed her mouth. The quiver of her chin. And wanted to pull her against him.

Not for sex.

Just to hold her and let her know she wasn't alone. He might even have done so if she hadn't suddenly said, "Now, no more lollygagging, Thomas.

You said you wanted to get through the rest of the rooms up here tonight, and with my sisters arriving tomorrow, I definitely need my beauty sleep."

Aware of the five other rooms needing their attention, Paige made it through the last of her shelves within the next half hour. Or rather, her perusal of his original shelves. He still had a few more to get through on her half.

"Look," she said, keeping in mind the passing time—and maybe needing to get some time alone to gather herself. Every time she was with West she ended up in some heavy-duty conversation with him, and she couldn't keep doing that.

Yeah, she was missing Walter—being in his home without him, meeting his son without him, taking care of the dogs without him, seeing the upstairs for the first time—and she was more than a little uncomfortable with her sisters' impending visit, but she'd dealt with far worse without getting all emotional or out of sorts.

He'd finally turned around to actually look at what she had to show him.

"Why don't we just go with... I'd like to own these two books?" She held up the two she'd picked, a fiction saga about two friends, and an encyclopedia of travel. "I'm willing to leave you with the entire rest of the collection, with the caveat that I can read any of them while I'm here, and we can get on to the other rooms." Fingers crossed they were as empty and devoid of personal belongings as the bedrooms along her hall.

"These books are up here." His response made no sense to her.

"Yeah."

"In my wing."

Oh.

She waited, thinking he'd realize that she'd hardly be invading his space by exchanging reads every now and then. And when he said nothing, she asked, "Are we being a little extreme here with our rules?"

"You want to worry about running into me all the time?"

Absolutely not. "No," she said, and then offered, "How about if I agree to visit this room only when I need something new to read, to let you know ahead of time that I'll be doing so and to only come in here when you're at the office, or otherwise out of the house?"

"What if you need something to read late at night?"

Really? "I'll visit the library downstairs or read something on my e-reader."

"Okay. Let's do the room across the hall." He climbed down off his ladder and headed for the door.

Leaving her to wonder why he was so bothered by the idea of her in his space at a time when he might actually be there. And late at night most of all.

Could it be because her presence was getting

to him, too? Could he be as attracted to her as she was to him?

And if so, what did she do about that?

Other than be just a tad bit more pleased than she should have been?

She'd take precautions, that's what. He was a stay-put kind of guy and she'd never be a woman who could do that. Which meant that anything developing between them would end in disaster. Worse than Lonnie, even. And the last thing either of them needed over the next year was another complication.

Weston had to hand it to Paige. When she had a job to do, she focused and got it done. They made it through four rooms in an hour—partially because, like the majority of the rooms in her hall, most of what they found was generic. Furnishings. Some rugs and bedding.

Most of which they determined to just leave as they were for the time being.

"This place is big enough for a husband and wife with grown, married kids and families of their own," she said as they left the fourth such room, heading down toward the last door on the floor. One that had been closed when he'd arrived the previous Friday and was still closed.

"Each married kid could get a wing and the husband and wife who started it all could have the center wing where Walter's room is."

Walter's room. He'd peeked in briefly, his first day in the place, and left the wing. There hadn't been time to go through his father's most personal things. Maybe he wasn't ready yet.

He heard Paige chattering behind him about cousins growing up on different wings as he opened the last door. In fact, he realized he'd grown a bit fond of her penchant for nonstop conversation over the past couple of hours as her innocuous thought processes had distracted him from the stirrings he'd been feeling, distancing him from some supposed connection to her that seemed at times to be almost beyond his control to stop.

It wasn't. He knew that. Just had to…

Door open, Weston stopped abruptly. Stared.

Paige's hand at his back kept him in the present. "What?" she asked, peering over his shoulder.

"I can't believe it," he said, feeling like an interloper as he stepped into the room, and yet wanting to be there and never leave, too. His dad's chair was there, the one that moved from their nicer home to the older one and sat in the same place in both living rooms. And a side table he also recognized, scratches and all.

The lamp on the table had been in his dad's bedroom when Weston was growing up. On his nightstand.

But the pictures…he could hardly take them in. "I've never seen most of these." Framed, sitting on the side table, filling a bookshelf around the television stand and completely covering three of the four walls, were pictures of his mom and dad. In a fishing boat. On a beach. In the home in which Weston started out his life. At a cabin someplace. Standing on a hill overlooking some huge body of water. And younger, at what looked like a school dance. An entire section of wall was given to wedding photos. And another section…

He drew closer, just studying. Many of the pictures were of his parents with him. Some just him and his dad. Some him and his mom. And some the three of them. Some were clearly snapshots. Some looked like they'd come from a professional photo shoot.

"I can't believe…" He hadn't seen any of them. Why on earth had his father not shown them to him?

Swallowing to offset the emotion closing his throat, he couldn't stop the sting of tears that filled his eyes. Blinked them back. Leaned in closer, seeing the love on his mother's face as she held him, and then with him when he was several months older, holding his hand. Helping him to stand on his own.

He was on his father's shoulders. And on what was clearly his first Christmas, his dad was handing him a plastic fishing pole.

The room was deathly still. Thinking himself alone, he turned to find that Paige hadn't quietly slipped away as he'd thought. She was standing in front of the wall that Walter's chair pointed at, moving from picture to picture. Taking time with each one. Seeming to study them all.

He could ask her to leave.

She wasn't hurting anything, though. Wasn't intruding on his private moment.

Turning back to the wall in front of him, he looked at all of the photos again, paying attention to facial expressions, finding nothing but joy there.

So why...

Paige, moving softly, appeared at the other end of his wall. There were more than fifty of these photos on just the one wall.

He was standing there, seeing them, and still couldn't take it all in. Her perusal brought her down the wall, closer to him, but he didn't move.

Wasn't sure where he went from there.

When she reached him, she didn't step too close. Didn't walk around him. And didn't speak, either.

She was just...there. A heart beating into his past. Into his emptiness.

"Have you seen these before?"

She shook her head. "He told me once that he didn't spend a lot of time with the home theater downstairs. That he had a room upstairs that he preferred... I thought at the time that it was because of the stairs…and the vastness of the house. Now I see why. He'd made a private haven for himself."

For himself.

Weston didn't get it.

He pictured his father sitting night after night in that room all alone, and still not saying anything to Weston about it or about the photos.

His father had always sounded so busy. Assuring Weston that he enjoyed coming home to Ohio to see him, rather than Weston coming to Atlanta. Almost as though Walter had wanted to keep this place to himself.

And yet… Weston approved of the room. Wanted it to remain exactly as it was. Knew he'd visit it again and again. There was no feeling of morbidity or loneliness there. Rather, the walls radiated a joy that filled the place.

A joy that seemed separate from him. "I've never seen these." The admission felt like a failure on his part. He'd been too removed…too judgmental…not enough of a son to provide his father with a safe place to share his deepest heart.

He should have spent time here.

He'd been relieved to have Walter come home to Ohio for their visits, rather than him having to take time off to travel down to Atlanta. It had made sense to him at the time. Walter was retired; he was not. And Walter still had a lot of friends in town that he'd seemed to enjoy visiting every time he'd come home.

Walter had been happy to visit Weston at home. He couldn't have reframed all of those memories.

After a moment of standing there silently, following his admission, Paige turned. "I'll be right back," she said before leaving the room.

She wasn't right back. He'd been all the way around the room, tried out his father's old chair and taken another turn around all three picture walls before he heard her flip-flops coming down the hall.

"Sorry," she said, bringing her usual flurry of energy with her as she entered the room. "It took me longer than I'd thought to find the right one. I thought it was one date, but it was another."

Given that he had no idea what she was talking about yet, he turned slowly, fingers tucked into the front pockets of his jeans, and saw the mini recorder in her hand. "Listen."

She pushed a button and before he could choose to do what she'd commanded or not, his father's voice filled the room.

It was too much. The room. The photos.

The voice.

But then... "Here's what I know about life. Great things happen That's what I know." His dad through and through.

"That's it? There's nothing else? No lessons you learned along the way?" Paige's recorded voice filled the room with double her essence, dizzying him.

Bothering him extra, at any rate.

Unsettling him with a confusing need to absorb some of her aura.

"That is the lesson." Walter's voice came again. "Great things happen."

"I don't get it." The words could have been his, but they weren't. Paige apparently had had the same response. "How is that a lesson?"

"If I told you bad things happen, I bet you'd get it. Probably nod your head with the strength of your understanding."

"Maybe." Her recorded chuckle touched him. Made him feel as though he wanted to know that woman. Glancing at her face in real time, he had a hard time putting the voice and the straight-faced, so serious female together. And yet, he could match the recorded voice with the woman who'd greeted him that first day.

Was she changing? Was he?

Paige was watching him.

Seeing too much?

He wanted to tell her to shut the thing off.

But like watching a train wreck, he couldn't turn away. Had to know.

"Bad stuff does happen," Walter continued after a long pause. And it held a tone Weston hardly recognized. His father had rarely sounded that serious.

Except when he'd called to tell Weston Rusty had passed in his sleep. And when he'd come to the hospital right after Mary died.

"It happens, and it hurts so badly you think you'd rather be dead, but the lesson is, great stuff happens. And will always happen again as long as you let go of the grief, forgive it for happening to you and put your energy, your choices, your will and your thoughts into getting to the next great thing."

"Forgive it for happening to you?"

Paige's recorded voice again, and Weston found himself fully engrossed.

"You ever forgive someone who did you wrong?" Walter had asked.

"Yeah."

"How'd it make you feel?"

"Better. It took away the sting of anger. And some of the hurt, too, probably."

"Same thing."

"But…"

"Nope, same thing. I'm not saying it's easy, forgiving bad stuff for happening. What I'm saying is that if you get there, you're that much closer to the great stuff."

"So…practically speaking, how do you go about forgiving a thing that happened?"

"You accept it. You accept that it happened. That it happened to you. You accept that it's part of your story. You acknowledge that you want to hold on to the great parts. Give yourself that license, and then you do what you have to do to move forward to the next great thing. Whatever it takes. Take my inventions. There were a lot of failures along the way. Some hurt worse than others. Maybe I had more invested in them financially, maybe I believed in them more. Those ones I tucked away. The ones that didn't bother me so much, I'd just pitch."

"I don't get it. If you're moving on, why keep the ones that bothered you the most?"

"Because those were the ones that helped me believe in more great things to come. Anytime you care deeply about something, it's a great thing. The deeper you care, the greater it is. And when it fails you, or you lose it, the more it hurts. So you tuck them away, lest the hurt prevent you from reaching the next great thing, but you hang on to them because if you don't you throw away the caring."

"Do you still have those failed prototypes?"

"I do."

"You ever look at them?"

"Are you kidding? Here in this house, the proof of my inventive success… I have them all around me. You see that lamp over there?"

"Yeah."

"Its base used to be a prototype for an affordable and light recyclable milk bottle. Probably would have worked, too, if I could have found the right formula of plastic to glass particles. I ran out of money and decided to cut my losses on that one. But I still think it could be done. Glass and plastic together, best of both worlds."

"And because of your success, the failure doesn't hurt anymore?"

"Because of my success, it's no longer a failure. It's a stepping stone to that success. And because I held on to them, they're all around me, those stepping stones. They're like companions, reminding me of who I am, all the parts of my getting here. And more than that, they fill my home with all of the caring I've been lucky enough to experience in my life. When they hurt, I had to put them aside so they didn't prevent me from moving on, but they were always there, they always had my back, with the lessons they taught me, the things they gave me, the things I gave them, and now, here I am, a happy man today because of all of them…"

He heard the recorder click off. Met the gaze of the woman who'd probably just given him the best gift he was ever going to get.

"He wasn't going to let his grief over losing her cloud the great thing she'd given him." Paige's words were almost like whispers on the air. "And those pictures…they made him hurt too badly…"

They couldn't know that for sure, but he believed she was right.

And knew, too, that his father had spent the last months of his life a genuinely happy man. Surrounded by the loves of his life.

Himself included.

Chapter Thirteen

Paige wasn't sure what to do next. She couldn't walk out on him. And wasn't sure he wanted her to stay.

Taking her cue from Walter, she tried to figure out the next great thing. Wanted so badly to run a hand along the side of Weston's face, to let him know that he wasn't alone.

Sometimes human beings just needed to be touched. Sometimes that was the only communication they could take in or understand.

But whether this moment was one of those times, or she just wanted it to be, didn't much matter. They had to get through a year being co-owners of the same house.

She couldn't touch him.

"I don't think your dad ever stopped looking for the next great thing or stopped creating the next great things in his life," she said, in lieu of the physical comfort she couldn't provide. "Look at the dogs, the kennel. He got so excited every time we got someone new in. Would always spend whatever time it took to make our newest addition comfortable, to feel welcome and wanted…"

Weston met her gaze, held on to it again, in a way that was becoming way too familiar. All of the things they couldn't say, or do, seemed to be wrapped up in that look.

"Thank you."

"For what?"

"Just for being you. For being available. For being there for my dad. For caring about his story, his life. For being a good person."

She shrugged, not so sure she deserved credit for all that. She'd been hired to do a job and she'd done it. And she'd made a one-year soul promise she had to keep.

He took a step closer. "Mostly, thank you for sharing it all with me. For giving me a second chance after the way I came on that first day. For sticking around when you didn't have to do so."

Needing to back up, quickly, she couldn't move her feet.

"I don't stick around." She didn't want to think about why it was so important, in that moment, that he understand that part. "I'm just not done here yet."

He nodded. Not seeming to be the least bit put off by her confession.

"And I'm being selfish here, too. I'm getting what I need out of the situation."

"What do you need?"

Oh, God. She needed to wet her lips. To feel his hands on her breasts. To…

"I need to find out what else your father has to teach me." She got the words out, finding them through the fuzziness West's closeness was creating in her brain.

"What else?"

"All of that you just heard, it wasn't just key to you. It changed my life, too."

"How so?"

If he'd just back up, look at her a little less intensely, it would be easier for her to tell him.

"He helped me understand myself. To find myself. For so long, as I traveled, I felt like something was wrong with me. Like I was programmed differently inside than most people. And then, when I spent time with your dad, listened to him, I knew that what I thought was wrong was the part of me that was the healthiest of all. My sisters want what happened in my past, with my parents, to define me. But it doesn't. It's a part of me, I take it with me, but I choose to find the good in life."

Mariah and Tess wouldn't let the past go. Always wanted to keep it front and center in their conversations with her. Convinced that she had buried issues that she had to deal with, or she'd never be happy.

They didn't get that she *was* happy.

Far happier than either of them, she'd guess. While they were both married, both seemed to spend far more time worrying about fixing her than getting on with their own lives.

The more she thought about them, and the inexplicable relationship she had with West, the more their presence at the estate made her nervous. She'd only ever had to deal with them in her own space. Alone.

Couldn't be sure that she could ward off every eventuality of a collision with West, as she couldn't know what might bring about those circumstances.

"Seriously, Weston…" She was particularly careful to use his full name. "If either of my sisters find you, or try to engage you in conversation, I need you to politely disengage yourself."

The abrupt change of topic wasn't subtle. She was drowning in his proximity. Had to distance herself, even if all she could use was conversation at the moment.

She still hadn't taken a single step away from him, and he didn't move back. Or blink.

"You have my word." He could have been vowing to love her until death did they part. Or at least that's the way she heard it.

She'd been underwater there with him for too long. Had to come up for air.

"I'm not running. I have nothing to run from," she blurted, thinking about what she'd learned from Walter. About how to save herself. To save her and West from crossing a line that would break them both.

"Anything that's happened in my life goes right

along with me. And I wouldn't have it any other way. The things that I've been through add up to make me who I am. And there's nothing in particular that I'm heading toward, either, other than new experiences. I just don't like to stay in one place for too long. I'm a wanderer, always wanting to learn more and to know what's out there that I haven't seen. I think that's why I like ghostwriting so much. I get to be exposed to so many different walks of life. My sisters don't get that."

She was rambling, and summing things up, too. Reminding both of them why they had to step back from each other. Reiterating that if her sisters got to him and tried to fill his head with some other version of her, it wouldn't be correct; they didn't know.

Reminding herself of who she was.

Who she was not.

What she could not…

His lips seemed to be coming closer. She lifted her head, just to see him more clearly, to verify her perception, felt the faintest brush of his mouth on hers and…

Dropped the tape recorder on her bare pinky toe.

He had to hand it to her. For a spell maker, Paige was also one hell of a spell breaker. He'd kissed quite a few women in his time, but had never had one jump and say "ouch!" before.

He'd barely touched Paige.

And still felt their heat burning through him as he bent to pick up what she'd let fall, taking a few steps back before reaching his arm all the way out to return her property to her.

"That...that can't happen," she said, her voice breaking a bit.

"Agreed." His wholehearted response didn't even begin to cover his feelings on the matter. He shoved his hands into his pockets, as far as the newly too tight jeans would allow, as if to put the period on the end of his sentence. "I apologize. I was out of line and I swear to you, I have never, in my life, kissed a woman with whom I wasn't on a date and without knowing for certain that I had permission to do so."

"We didn't really kiss."

Tell his body that. His lips were still tingling from that faint brush. "Thanks to you," he allowed. What in the *hell* had he been thinking?

He hadn't been thinking. Which wasn't like him at all. He was the guy who always overthought every move he was about to make.

And then thought about it once more before actually making the move.

"I dropped the recorder by accident."

Always honest, Paige. He did admire that about her.

"And you have no reason to apologize," she continued, which was also the way she operated. He was growing accustomed to her. "I know full well

I was sending out the invitation, though it's kind of you to spare my feelings and not point that out."

She'd been sending out vibes?

She'd been sending out vibes.

It wasn't just him.

And…his body couldn't help reacting when a beautiful woman came on to him, right? Could explain some of his odd reaction to her, those vibes she'd been sending.

Didn't explain, or in any way condone, his body getting away from him. That absolutely could not happen again. A man could feel desire, but he had to, at all times, be in full control of what he did with those feelings.

Walter had made that fact clear to him long before West had even known what his father was talking about. Because as frivolous as his father might have been at times, he'd raised his boy to have high values and to always respect others.

"So…we need another rule," he said. "Boundaries firmly established, so our near miss doesn't come close to an explosion. Ever."

"Agreed."

"I say, for now, we put off going through the rest of the house. We've each got our own wing. We've set up guidelines by which you can access the library up here."

She nodded.

"And we limit the time we spend together," he

added. "We can set up a schedule and alternate dog feedings where we're alone, just like we plan to while your sisters are here. With the exception of at least two days a week, being in there together with them so the pups are used to more than one person in their midst at a time. Because animals' adoptive families often have more than one person." He was getting the hang of parts of his new life, at least.

Her response was another affirmative head bob. A step back. Tapping her recorder on the palm of her hand. And when he suddenly drew a blank, thinking about the near kiss that recorder had interrupted, she said, "And we need to set up a communication process. I'd prefer text message. It allows instant dispersal of knowledge, as much as a phone call, and yet isn't as intrusive."

He liked the sound of that. Thought about the business he was just getting up and running.

"We should have some kind of meeting schedule as well. Separate from the dogs so that we can focus. Say, at the kitchen table. Once a week. Times to be determined on a week-by-week basis, but never over a meal."

"Good. That sounds good." She took another step backward, toward the door.

"And we should have separate laundry days," he added. He was generally a throw-in-a-load-as-needed type of guy, but he hadn't shared laundry facilities since college. "I take my shirts and pants to the cleaners, but do the rest…"

Too much information.

"I'd rather just say I have morning use of the facilities and you have evening use." She quickly butted in as he fell silent.

Saving his butt again. Maybe their plan to get through the next year unharmed really was going to work.

The feeling of euphoria that brought had him offering her a smile. "We make pretty damned good business partners," he told her, considering that, working together, they'd just avoided implosion.

Or maybe not. As a clouded look crossed her face, one he didn't recognize, he waited for her to say something. And when she didn't, had to ask, "What's wrong?"

Communication was key. They'd just made that a rule.

"I just…partners…you know… I travel solo and all…"

Ah, right. He did, too, since Mary, but that wasn't professional conversation. "Business partners," he reiterated. "We just run the same train. With you in one car and me in the other."

He was beginning to see the wealth in his father's philosophy. Looking to the next great thing. They could each take their pasts into the future they each wanted, with the one-year investment.

They had an understanding. A plan to make it work.

They were going to succeed.

"I like that," she said. "We're running a train and have our separate cars. That analogy…it's so creative of you…"

She smiled. He smiled. Their eyes met.

And didn't let go.

Until she turned and practically ran from the room. Leaving him alone in the room with the quagmire of emotions they'd let loose in there.

Could be he'd taken his victory lap eleven months and twenty-five days too soon.

Chapter Fourteen

For all her worry, Paige's time with her sisters turned out to be the most enjoyable of any she could remember. They'd made their mama's chili and party casserole, spent a lot of time in the home theater watching girlie movies, shopped and, when West was at work, spent time in the pool.

She'd known the pool was just off from the dining room French doors. Had seen the bill for the guy who came each week to maintain it, and the expansive cool decking around it. But she hadn't even thought about actually venturing out and using it until Tess had suggested that they do so. She'd wanted to go out every day since then, and, most days, did manage to get in a half hour or so.

Mariah had wanted to help her get settled in her suite upstairs and they'd bought a throw rug, curtains, and moved a desk and chair in from one of the unused rooms down her hall. And as a gift to her, her sisters purchased a large monitor and docking station for her laptop so that she didn't have to strain her eyes so much when she spent hours writing.

It wasn't the type of possession she could take

with her when she left, but she'd been enjoying its use in the meantime.

And, as she'd known they would, they fell in love with the dogs. What she hadn't expected was that Mariah wanted to adopt Erin, and when they found out that the female pug just made the cabin carry-on requirements, arrangements were finalized so that Erin could go with them.

She and her sisters had talked heart to heart a bit, too, but they hadn't harped at all on her lifestyle this time. Her career choice. Or her future. Of course, they'd had no reason to do so. They thought she was finally settling down.

She couldn't tell them that she'd only be co-owner of Walter's estate for a year. On a hunch, that Wednesday morning before they'd arrived, after she'd called the contractors about building a second kennel room and pen, she'd phoned Grant Lieberman regarding the will and what she should tell her siblings about her current situation. Grant had suggested that, as verbal agreements could sometimes be legally binding, she shouldn't have any mention of one on record anywhere, including with family members.

He'd also told her that, in light of the siblings she had that Walter hadn't known about, if she was adamant about protecting West's future rights, she should have a trust drawn up, naming him as full beneficiary of her half of the estate. Walter hadn't known she had other beneficiaries who could, conceivably, contest Walter's right to determine her beneficiary, if she, in fact, had been in full compliance with his addendums at the time of her death.

She'd instructed him to draw up a trust immediately and had already signed it.

Mariah and Tess had lamented their inability to catch West around, at all. Paige knew, from the text he'd sent, that he'd decided to head to Ohio during their visit, to finalize details there, and get the rest of his things packed up and on a moving truck.

She'd wondered if he'd had a female friend at home, someone he'd spent time, maybe nights, with. Wondered if she'd been a "detail" and the finalization was that the woman would be visiting him in Atlanta. When the thought kept interrupting her time with her sisters and brought with it an accompanying sadness, she banished them both.

He'd said he was never going to marry. Walter had told her, and worried incessantly, that West hadn't been serious with a woman since his fiancée's death, but it was turning out that there were many things Walter didn't know about his son.

Or hadn't shared.

And West's love life, or lack thereof, was absolutely none of her business or concern.

West had taken the full five days away allotted to him for the month. The exact number of days her sisters had been there. But he'd texted with her each day. Approving the contractor's bid for the new kennel and adding his signature to hers on the work order.

When he'd returned that Sunday, they'd both been cordial, sharing only that their weekends had gone fine. He'd missed saying goodbye to Erin and she'd told him her sister would be sending pictures each week.

She'd been careful to avoid looking him directly in the eye, had been secretly glad to have him home and had dreamed about him that night.

An X-rated dream.

They'd fed the dogs together that first evening he was back, but had settled into the routine they'd discussed, meeting together in the kitchen once a week to go over house accounts and discuss any estate business. And they met together for feeding time in the kennel twice a week, with their attention firmly on the pets.

Didn't stop her from getting wet down below just thinking about him. And didn't stop the sound of his voice from sending delicious shivers through her body sometimes.

They texted every day, usually just to affirm that dog time had happened and all was fine. Sometimes there was more. She'd offered him leftovers when she'd made pulled pork and let him know when there were a couple kinds of homemade soup in the freezer. He'd availed himself of both, but otherwise didn't seem to be using the kitchen at all.

She'd made a couple visits to the upstairs library, both with notice given, and had left notes of the books she'd taken as though she was checking them out of a public library.

All in all, their plan was working almost perfectly. A loner by all accounts, she loved her days at the house, but missed seeing other people, too. Thought maybe if she saw others more often, she'd be cured of her intense desire for her business partner. In clothes and without. She didn't have close friends—she never hung around any one place long enough to build tight-knit relationships—but she'd always lived in apartment complexes with people coming and going, familiar faces she'd smile at and offer "good mornings" to. She generally ate out more and got to know a waitress or a cook at some local diner or other.

And she'd always been a peripheral part of whatever family had employed her. Walter, for instance. He'd been her companionship for the first several months of her current job.

Now she just had his house.

And the dogs. They were her saving grace.

Still, when she'd found herself thinking of West first thing in the morning, and last thing at night, when she looked forward to heading to the kennel in the mornings after he'd been there, to smell the scent of his cologne, she'd taken charge. She'd just needed to get out of the house, get out into the world, and had joined a gym. And started volunteering at a women's shelter as well. Exercise kept her energy level high. And the volunteer work…was fulfilling beyond what she'd imagined.

Something new to add to her list of musts in her life. No matter where she was, she must find a shelter and volunteer.

They received a new pup the first week of their second month together. Angel was estimated to be between four and six months, but no one really knew for sure. She'd been found, near death, in the back of an abandoned puppy mill. She wouldn't be adoptable until she could be spayed, but the vet hadn't wanted to put her under anesthetic until her numbers were stable and she'd gained some weight. Because of the specialized care she'd need, Walter's kennel had been the first placement attempt they'd made.

Paige had called her a little angel when she'd first seen her, via a Zoom meeting, and following that call, the rescue counselor had written "Angel" as the dog's name on all her paperwork.

They couldn't be sure, but best educated guess, agreed upon by all involved, said that Angel was probably a full-breed cocker spaniel. If her numbers stabilized, indicating no permanent organ damage, her prognosis for a full healthy life was promising.

"Either she won't make it, or she'll be immediately adopted once she's put up," Paige told West as they drove together to the vet's office with Annie at the end of their fifth week of being co-owners of the estate.

West drove so Paige could hold Annie, who was going in for a six-week follow-up, per rescue regulations. Several veterinarians volunteered time for the rescues, and Dr. Doris Henderson, Annie's vet, was one Paige had never met.

"She'll make it," West said, referring to Angel, and driving as he did everything else—with precision, focus and strict adherence to the laws. The way he was riding the speed limit exactly really annoyed her. She didn't overtly break the law, ever, always staying within five miles per hour of the limit, but to stay exact like that...

Focusing on his speed was about the only thing she could find to take her mind off his hands on the wheel. His thighs closer to hers than they'd been in the past month. The slightly evergreen scent of his aftershave.

Glomming onto speed limits and traffic were also distracting her from worrying about Annie. She wasn't a vet and didn't have a scale in the kennel, but she was pretty sure that Annie hadn't gained any weight.

And rescues who couldn't be adopted didn't generally have good fates. It was all part of the system.

And if Annie was suffering, then maybe it'd be for the best if her misery was not prolonged. But the poodle/bichon mix didn't seem unhappy. She licked Paige's hand as Paige started to pet her. One delicate lick, but it was enough.

"We don't know that she'll make it," she said. They were still talking about Angel, officially. He hadn't mentioned Annie's appointment since she'd first texted him about it and he'd asked that it be scheduled at a time when he could be there, too.

"She's a pup, Paige. Unless she already had something wrong with her at birth, chances are good she'll pull through. There's no sign of internal bleeding or broken bones. All she needs is some good care and a chance to get stronger. Dogs are resilient. And adaptable."

She hugged Annie a little closer, nodded and directed him into the lot and where to park based on the instructions she'd been given.

He offered to carry Annie in, but she chose to do so. Whatever the appointment might bring, Annie was going to know she was loved.

Because they were receiving volunteer care, they had to wait for the time the doctor was free. While Paige walked with Annie—around the waiting room, outside, and around the room some more—West sat and read a magazine.

As irritating as his calmness was, she also found

his presence soothing. What would be, would be. She knew that.

She always knew that.

And she wasn't afraid of death. Not for herself or anyone she loved. Death was a guaranteed part of life.

Still, when they were called back, and West reached for Annie, she handed the little dog over to him. He didn't seem the least bit concerned about Annie rubbing her face between his forearm and his side, leaving a mark on his light blue dress shirt.

Paige had a similar mark on the white peasant blouse she'd put on that morning. Annie's eyes were tearing and, Paige assumed, were itching some.

The exam itself took about as much time as it had taken them to walk from where they'd waited down the hall to the exam room. Maybe a little more. Didn't seem that way to Paige. Dr. Henderson took time to study the chart the tech had filled in as she'd weighed the dog and taken her temperature.

"I wish I had better news," Doris Henderson, her gray hair back in a bun, said. Her dark eyes grave, she continued, "While she's not exhibiting any signs of severe disease, Annie's not showing any indication of weight gain, and without that, I can't safely recommend adoption. She's got an eye infection as well, which would need drops, twice daily, maybe indefinitely."

"Would the drops make her eyes more comfortable?" West asked the question on the tip of Paige's tongue. He stood directly across from the doctor at the exam table, one hand on the side of Annie's neck. Just holding her. Letting Annie know he was there.

Watching that hand, Paige felt a pang of emotion she hadn't known in her entire adult life. Far more than fondness, than caring... Her heart locked on West.

The sensation passed. She could breathe easier again. And she knew she was just reacting to the recommendation she knew was coming.

Before Dr. Henderson could say anything more, Paige asked, "Can you give us just a second, Doctor?"

Shooting the two of them a look of compassion, the doctor nodded.

Before the door even closed behind her, shutting them alone in the room for the first time, Paige, standing her ground in the far corner, blurted out, "I think we should adopt her."

He looked at Annie, and then up at her. "If she's not able to gain weight, we might just be prolonging the inevitable."

She shrugged. Stuck her chin up. "And your point is?"

"What difference will it make if it's now or six weeks from now?"

"Six weeks of love and joy."

"Okay, say we adopt her and she makes it, just takes extra care for the rest of her life, and she's still around when your year is up. What then? You're going to be better able to say goodbye to her?"

She could always say goodbye. That ability was a very delicate and cherished talent she'd mastered.

"I know how to do that, yes," she said, looking at the dog, who chose that moment to look over at Paige. Probably because she'd just heard Paige's voice. "But…um… I was thinking…maybe I'd take her with me. You've got Checkers. I'll take Annie. I can always get a place that allows pets."

She hadn't actually consciously thought the idea through. But maybe, in the back of her mind, it had been brewing. She certainly had answers ready as he asked her questions.

"You just going to leave her alone in an apartment all day while you go off to work?"

"I work from home a lot. And when I'm gone, I can hire someone to look after her."

"She's not good with strangers. That's part of the problem."

"We haven't had her long enough to know how she'll acclimate in the long run. And if she doesn't get any better at it, then I'll leave her with you, in the environment she knows. And you make whatever decision you have to make regarding her future at that time."

She traveled light. And never with anything that needed her attention. But maybe it was time to change that. Life was all about change. About new experiences.

And having a warm body next to you, having a mouth to feed other than your own...it was nice. She'd always had an affinity with dogs.

The more she thought about the idea, the more it grew on her.

Whether West got that she wasn't going to back down or he agreed with her, she didn't know. But then minutes later, as he carried Annie out of the vet's office and put her on Paige's lap in the front seat of his car, they had Dr. Henderson's signature on the privately funded Operation Rescue's adoption papers.

Annie officially belonged to them.

Or would as soon as the paperwork was filed and complete.

Checkers and Annie were now brother and sister.

Paige smiled, thinking she was starting to understand why Walter had arranged the partnership between her and his son.

West had let Checkers into his heart. And she'd found a place in her life for Annie. A way to be free to roam and still have a family of her own.

As long as West kept his delectable body away from her as well as he'd been doing, they were going to survive the year and get on with the rest of their lives just fine.

Chapter Fifteen

With Annie and Angel both needing special care, and with Angel just learning to trust the two of them, West and Paige agreed to pair up for feeding time over the next few days. They'd both separately done a lot of reading, sending each other links to pertinent articles, and had determined, since Annie was theirs and not being groomed to enter a new household, they would no longer adhere to their rescue protocol in terms of feeding. They started mixing in small amounts of various table food protein to her meals, thinking that differing smells might keep her minute amount of interest piqued. Paige scrambled eggs, boiled chicken, broiled lamb, shredded cheese and Annie ate about as much, as little, as she normally did.

On the third morning, Paige, in a long tight-fitting denim skirt, beneath an enticingly form-fitting brown short-sleeved top, lay on the floor next to Annie's bowl. With her head propped on one hand, her luscious, unbelievably long hair flowing all over the floor around her, she was hand-feeding the dog.

He might have gotten lost in the sight if Angel hadn't just stepped on the edge of her bowl, making a noise loud enough to draw his attention.

Their newest family member had finished her breakfast of moistened puppy food. She looked about ready to nod off as West grabbed her up off the floor, still monitoring as the other dogs ate, to make sure no one jumped bowls. Until the puppy was able to play, to hold her ground, they'd been advised to keep her away from the bigger dogs and had gated off a portion of the room for her.

When Paige was in the room during the day, which was pretty much every day since they'd taken in Angel, she'd have Angel up on the couch with her. In between trips outside. The little pup hadn't come to them potty-trained, either, but Paige was already making headway there.

She was a natural mother. The vision of her with a flock of her own, canine and human, came to him so clearly, he shook his head.

She was such a natural nurturer. A person, seemed to him, made for parenting.

And if he was right, she had no idea how the future was going to knock her on the head. He didn't know when. He didn't know where. But it would catch up to her. Either with regret, when she was older and childless, or with joy, if she figured herself out in time to have her own family.

Where the frivolous idea came from, he had no

idea. Probably just from him breathing her air. Or from him being so completely in lust with her that he was creating a fantasy that could never be, just to tide himself over until the temptation moved on, out of his life.

A woman in his life permanently, or a houseful of kids, were definitely not fantasies he would want, so it seemed right that his mind would conjure it up. Give him a vision of something he didn't want to displace that one thing he did.

Paige Martinson naked in his bed.

Naked anywhere within touching distance of him.

Abe was the first one to finish eating. He'd filled out nicely during the weeks they'd had him, hardly resembling the skinny little bedraggled terrier West had first met. West had him figured for the next one to find a forever home.

Standing there, watching Annie's delicate little tongue take a bit of dog food off Paige's finger, West somehow segued the vision to himself eating out of her hand and almost got hard.

A state of affairs that intensified when that vision transformed into one where her fingers were touching his mouth oh so softly.

All of the together time they'd been having the past few days was clearly taking a negative toll on his ability to successfully manage their unusual business partnership.

Checkers was the last one to finish eating and still Paige lay with Annie, getting a bite or two in her every few minutes. They'd tried leaving Annie up in Paige's room with a full bowl of food the day before, thinking the dog might want to graze all day, but all she'd done was sleep by the door. Didn't eat or drink for the hours she was there.

Paige didn't lose patience, though. At least not that he could see. She spoke softly, encouragingly, as though she had all day to lie on the hard cement floor with goo on the end of her finger.

And he was reminded of a time the previous week when she'd been showing him another slew of pictures that Mariah had sent of Erin. It had been like she'd been a proud mama, or aunt, the expression on her face as she'd looked at the photos again with him. And he remembered something else, the way she'd scrolled a couple of photos too far. One of the very next pictures in her phone's gallery and been of Stover—the German shepherd who'd left the day after he'd arrived.

"What?" Her tone not quite as soft, and more challenging, she was looking straight at him.

Frowning, he shook his head. Checked to make sure that Angel was still sleeping, her little head tucked into his armpit. "What, what?"

"You were looking at me like you had some kind of secret and smiling that weird little smile you had right before you told me you'd chosen the flooring for the new kennel without consulting me. I don't like things going on behind my back. Hate any surprise aimed in my direction, actually. And especially one from a business partner."

He hadn't realized he'd been smiling. But figured honesty was the only way out of the current hot water he'd managed to wade into. "You talk a great talk about wanting to wander the globe alone, but you're falling in love there. No way you're going to be able to just say goodbye and leave her behind."

Which meant they had a little over ten months to get the dog well enough to travel the globe with her.

Ten long months of cold showers and libido maintenance.

"Of course, I'll be able to say goodbye." She sat up, her legs curled around the right side of her butt. And there he'd been trying not to notice that enticing part of her anatomy. She had to go and make her feet point it out to him...

"It's one of my talents. Something I'm actually good at. Some people really struggle with goodbye, have a hard time dealing with it. I don't." Her shrug reinforced her confident tone.

He still wasn't sure he was buying it.

"That's because your lifestyle doesn't really allow you to have a tribe," he said, more to challenge her than because he had any idea what he was talking about.

"Of course I have a tribe. Everyone does, whether

they know it or not. I'm very self-aware, West. And self-honest, too. Maybe because I had to be. Maybe because I just chose to be. Either way, I'm good."

She honestly *sounded* good. And something pushed him to push her. Not necessarily a good something. Her complacence seemed to challenge his own well-being, though that made no logical sense to him.

"Who's your tribe?" he asked, looking for a way to get through her formidable armor.

"My parents. The grandmother who raised me and my sisters after the…accident. Our dog at the time, Zelda. Your dad. The first woman I ever wrote for. We'd met at a college mixer, a formal fund-raising event that my professor had invited me to attend. She hired me as a ghostwriter on the spot. And her memoir went straight to the top of a number of bestseller lists."

"So that's why you're financially comfortable."

She cocked her head, then shrugged. "I don't usually get royalties, if that's what you mean. And I'm not credited with the writing. She did pay me a handsome fee, and then an incredibly generous bonus when the book did so well."

"What was the name of the book?"

She told him and he was shocked.

"Abigail Anderson? The woman who was one of the early tech pioneers? I read she did her work under an assumed male name so the field would pay attention?"

Abigail Anderson had been legendary in her later years. And had lived to be almost a hundred. She'd passed about a year after her book hit the stands.

"Yeah."

"I'm impressed."

"Don't be. Abigail was actually a great writer. I just helped her organize her thoughts into chapters and wrote transition scenes, and toward the end a chapter or two."

"You have a recent picture of Stover on your phone. Right along with Erin. You don't just walk away."

West smiled at her.

Their eyes met. Held.

He wondered why he hadn't met her sooner in his life.

Wondered how he could just plain like one woman so much more than any other he'd ever known.

She looked away and he lurched, felt her absence like a jab to the gut, knew she'd done the right thing.

And wasn't ready to let her go, now or in ten months.

"So, back to your tribe. Everyone you've named, to my knowledge, and by age calculation, is gone."

"Yeah."

"What about your sisters?"

"They're more like a neighboring tribe."

Did everything about her have to be so damned interesting to him? "I don't get it."

"It's simple, really." She stood, picking Annie up and a half-empty bowl with her. "We're all going to die. It's a fact of life that most people avoid. It scares a lot of them. But it doesn't scare me. I'm looking forward to getting to the other side, where there is no death. And where I'll be reunited with those I've lost."

He wasn't about to get into a philosophical discussion with a woman who'd had to process losing both parents suddenly at the age of eleven. Was kind of impressed with how she'd worked it all out, though.

"Is that why you seem to surround yourself with older people and dogs? Because they'll likely get there before you and you'll have a huge tribe waiting for you?"

Her look intensely serious, she cocked her head, took a step toward him. Stopped. "I can't believe you just said that."

"What? I'm just..." He didn't know what. Being logical with the facts presented, he supposed.

"You're the first person I've ever known who actually gets it," she said. And then continued with "And now you know why I don't have a problem saying goodbye."

"Because for you, it's only 'see you later.'"

"Right."

Something drove him to not to leave it at that.

Something strong within him. Like he was suffocating and needed air.

"But maybe there's more."

"What more?"

"I don't know." He truly didn't. "Just seems like if you live your whole life for the final future, you're wasting the now, and maybe that future would be better for you if you have 'nows' in the past when you get there."

He was in too deep. Never, ever had he had conversations like the one he was having with her.

And yet he just stood there. Didn't do anything to get himself out.

"It sounds to me like maybe you need to get to work and straighten out numbers for a while," she said, smiling at him in a playful way that completely took his mind off their words, and focused it firmly on her lips. And the body that went with them.

"Sleep with me."

She didn't say no.

She didn't *say* anything. Her dark blue eyes wide with a rumble of emotion, she just looked at him.

"I can't be imagining everything," he said. "It's between us, like a living entity."

She didn't deny it.

"So why not let it run its course?" The suggestion was from left field. And yet, as he voiced it, the idea was familiar. As though he'd known for a while.

"In some ways, it's the perfect solution," he told

her. Not to convince her of anything. But to speak a truth that seemed to be determined to be heard. The way it kept taking them by surprise, no matter how hard they both tried to pretend it wasn't there.

Or to distract themselves from it.

"In what ways?" Her voice sounded dry, croaky. And he got hard.

"I don't have to worry about the fact that I don't want marriage or entanglement. Because you don't, either. And you don't have to worry about being trapped, or fearing that I might get too close, because… I don't want the entanglement."

She licked her lips. "What you're saying is, we want the same things."

Yeah. He nodded. That was what he was saying. And he felt pretty certain that he was right.

She couldn't believe she was doing this. Having the conversation. Flirting with the idea of having sex with West.

More than flirting with the idea. She was actually considering it.

"It's getting harder to avoid," she said aloud. "And exhausting, having to work so hard at it all the time. And it hasn't even been two months yet." With ten more stretching out after that. Her crotch had been wet since he'd asked her to sleep with him. Her nipples were hard and her breasts actually ached. The swirling in her groin was the worst, though. She needed release.

The kind only he could give her.

"You'd have to put Angel down."

Annie had already gone over to lie down in her usual spot.

He nodded. Didn't move. But the look in his eye—there was no doubt he was dead serious.

And a glance at his jeans told her how ready he was.

"I want you," he told her, and even though she already knew that, his words sent a rigid thrill of desire through her.

She nodded. "I know."

"You want me, too."

"Desperately." What was the point in denying it? Still, he held the sleeping puppy.

"Maybe we need some rules," she suggested. They seemed to do well with agreed-upon boundaries.

A light came to his eyes, just as she'd known it would. "What would you suggest?"

She almost smiled, but answered his question instead. "Do we limit the number of times a week?"

Frowning, he said, "I don't see much point in that. Do you?"

"No." But the idea of having at least a modicum of self-control might be a good one.

"Oh, I have one," she blurted as another thought occurred to her. "We each spend the night in our own beds. Alone."

Coming up with a list of rules for having sex was turning out to be quite sexy. But then, everything involving West Thomas turned her on.

"That's a good one," he agreed. "I concur. And we don't let it change the rest of our relationship. We're still business partners. None of the emotional attachments people seem to bring to sex." He was nodding as he finished the sentence and looked straight at her.

"Agreed. But I took that as a given."

"Then scratch that one. We don't need it."

"And birth control." Always a rule for her. "I have condoms, if you don't. I can't take the pill. I had a blood clot when I was younger."

Birth control. Because his…was going to be inside her. She was hot down there; her knees were weak.

When his gaze narrowed, she heard her last statement again and knew what had distracted him, and quickly added. "It was nothing. The result of an injury, but that's one of the questions before you're cleared to take the pill and…"

"I have condoms," he said. "But it's good that you do, too, in case we end up in your room."

"They're in my bag." Which went everywhere with her. Was currently on the couch. His gaze immediately turning in that direction, he gently put Angel in her pen, grabbed her bag, headed toward the door and turned back to look at her.

"You coming?"

Hell yes, she was coming.

And he hadn't even touched her yet.

Chapter Sixteen

The second she was within reach, West's lips went straight for Paige's. Standing in the doorway of the kennel, he lifted both hands to the sides of her face and opened his mouth on hers, meeting her tongue to tongue without taking a breath.

Driven by the acute ache inside him, all he could do was find the relief she'd given him permission to seek.

Or so he thought.

When she groaned against his lips, he had another goal. To make her do it again.

And again.

And again.

He had to bring her that much pleasure, or he'd never be satisfied.

When Darcy came up and nosed West's calf, Paige pulled West out of the room, and managed to close the kennel door. He had her pressed against the washer the very next second, his erection grinding erotically into her pelvis bone. Her hands scoured his shoulders and, needing to feel those fingers on his bare skin, he wanted to rip off his shirt.

He went for hers instead, sliding his hands beneath it to find a thin wispy bra. With one quick pinch the fastener was undone and he broke his lips from hers only long enough to drag both bra and shirt up over her head in one motion.

He'd meant to bring his lips right back to her mouth, but was distracted by the glorious, pale white mounds he'd exposed.

"I'll let you play with them if you take me someplace more comfortable," she told him. "And lose your shirt along the way."

It was a challenge he couldn't refuse.

Paige rode a wave of euphoria unlike anything she'd ever known. Physically, she was alight with sensation that flowed rapidly, continuously through her. No part of her was untouched, inside or out.

The sexual desire she recognized. The rest, it raged more powerfully than her own understanding. She went with it, couldn't fight it, didn't even want to try, and when West stumbled with her to the couch in the formal living room, she had no thought but to be naked with him, skin to skin, and then joining their bodies in the age-old ritual that was a part of life.

The first coming together, his sliding inside her, took her breath completely. She soared to the heavens, what she'd known they'd be, saw gold and light and then stars as sensation riveted through her in waves. Her last conscious thought before that had been when she'd grabbed a condom from her purse as he pulled one from his wallet and they raced to get one on him.

From there to him inside her and orgasm was a blip in time.

He'd been there first and sent her immediately sailing over the highest precipice.

"Wow." She was underneath him, with him still inside her, when she floated slowly back to earth. "You think that was so powerful because we waited so long?"

"I think we waited so long that we have to do it again, to relieve the pressure," he told her, pulling out of her to stand, and lifting her onto her feet, and walking with her toward his staircase. "My bed because it's closer," he told her with a long kiss, leaning against the staircase wall as he started to plunge into her a second time.

"New condom," she said, even as her body moved to accommodate him, and they somehow made it upstairs, did the necessary housework in less than a minute and were on his sheets with him inside her, her moving on top of him.

The second time was no less sensational than the first.

The third also.

They moved together, exploring, touching, entering, until she was too exhausted to keep her eyes open. They drifted shut, right there on his pillow, and then, she remembered.

She couldn't sleep in his bed.

"I have to go," she mumbled, grabbing a shirt out of his closet and pulling it on to the sound of his moan.

She wanted him to ask her stay, even though she knew she wouldn't.

He stood instead, all muscled manliness, and walked with her to the door. "No regrets," he told her, leaning against the jamb, his hand pushing her hair behind her ear and then running along the length of the strand down to her hip. His touch was delicious, and she melted some.

"That's what rules are for," she whispered. "To protect us against regrets."

Bending down slowly, he kissed her. Gently. And passionately, too. "A promise for later."

She liked that. Smiled at him. "I'm going to hold you to that, you know."

"I'm counting on it."

He kissed her again. She kissed him back. And turned to go.

"Sleep well, partner."

His words, following her softly down the hall, pierced her gently.

She had no regrets where he was concerned.

The yearlong partnership was looking more doable than ever. More pleasurable than ever.

She'd finally met a man who could live in the moment with her and not get burned.

Over the next month they had sex almost every day. Sometimes, on weekends, more than once a day. As time passed, West was amazed at how well their unusual partnership was working. Other than the sex, nothing had changed. They spent no more time together than they had before. Held their weekly meetings, and fed the dogs on schedule, sometimes together, sometimes not.

Checkers slept in his room with him.

Annie was in hers, for the time being. An experiment to see if the dog would find confidence in the privilege.

They both tended to Angel as necessary and while the dog was gaining some weight, her appetite was intermittent and there were concerns about her lack of energy.

And while Buddy still didn't come running up to greet them, the cocker mix hadn't peed inside for a couple of weeks.

And Darcy. She'd been approved for adoption. They expected her to be leaving them. West was going to miss the friendly dog and was also glad that Darcy would have a forever home where she'd be the center of attention.

Paige reported having finished his father's memoir, rough and final drafts, and sent it off to the publisher without any outside reads, per Walter's wishes. She was in the process of reviewing offers for future projects.

He let her know, via text mostly, as his build-out was completed, and when he hired an accountant and receptionist to work with the secretary he'd hired early on. And when he received and accepted a request to handle all accounting needs for a second national client as well.

She continued to cook, and occasionally, but not so often he knew when to expect it, text him that there were leftovers in the refrigerator or extras in the freezer. And he continued to eat out every meal that she didn't provide for him on their shared property.

They ate no meals together, not counting the chocolate and whipped cream that had made it onto their bodies, and they never ever went out together.

They weren't dating.

They were enjoying a perk to joint estate ownership, while the "joint" part lasted.

He'd never enjoyed a perk so much. Had never had such a lusty appetite.

Had never, ever even imagined sitting in his office at work, thinking about ways to lose himself in long tresses of hair, how to get parts of his body tangled up in them, so she'd use her delicate fingers to set him free.

The woman brought out a colorful streak in him he'd never met before.

And, for a time, because he knew it was temporary, he was letting himself go with it.

At some point the newness would wear off. He
knew that. It was a fact of life. And when that happened for him and Paige, they'd move on.

With no regrets.

When it would happen, he had no idea. Didn't
worry about it, trusting that it would happen long
before their year was up.

Maybe when they could be around each other,
outside of meetings and dog feedings, and keep
their hands off each other, they'd actually get
through more rooms in the house, going through
his father's stuff.

Walter's things weren't going anywhere and West
kind of took comfort from living among them just
as his father had.

As time passed, though, and his body benefitted
daily from Paige's generous and expressive nature,
he grew more curious about her ex, whom she'd
mentioned once, in the beginning. Weston had challenged her about not having met the right guy yet,
and she'd said she had met him. But that she didn't
believe in making promises she couldn't keep.

He got the promises thing now, but still wondered about this other person. How had he fared
when Paige had been done with him?

How did she treat a man once it was over?

The fact that the time was coming didn't bother
him, but not knowing how it would play out started

to. He just wanted to know. To be prepared. In case things petered out for her before they did for him.

Reminding himself that one of their ground rules had been established around the importance of communication, he decided to bring the matter up at a weekly meeting at the kitchen table one Wednesday.

They never had a formal agenda, but one or the other of them brought a list of discussion items occasionally. Or bills to peruse. He'd continued to keep the estate books, and he reported on them every single week, even if just to say there was no change.

He wasn't sure how to broach the "right man" topic. Another rule, to which they'd strictly adhered, was no personal conversation unless the other brought it up first.

And…she had brought it up…

Trying not to be distracted by the skintight bright orange, red and yellow tie-dyed shirt she'd worn to the meeting with a pair of yellow balloon pants, he saved the conversation for the new-business portion of the meeting.

"We set no statute of limitations on how long after someone had instigated personal conversation, we could bring it up again."

"Would you like to do so now?"

It would be easier if she'd tie back that hair. The way it flowed around her shoulders and onto the back of the chair wasn't business-meeting-like as it wasn't conducive to thoughtful conversation.

"Yes," he said firmly. And then, because when

he sought the right words they didn't come, he less professionally blurted, "Whatever happened to the right man for you?"

"Excuse me?" She frowned, seeming genuinely confused as opposed to angry. "I thought we were talking about statutes of limitations. Setting them."

"No, we're talking about a personal conversation you brought up that I wanted to speak to."

"As I recall, I didn't bring Lonnie up. You did."

Lonnie? The specter of the guy seemed to grow right there at the table with them. "How could I bring up someone I didn't even know existed?"

"You said I'd just never met the right man. We'd been talking about relationships. I responded with the fact that I had met him, but that I..."

"Wouldn't make promises you couldn't keep," he finished for her, to prove that he remembered, in an effort to take back control of a conversation he needed to have. "And now you've said his name is Lonnie." As if that proved something.

"His name *is* Lonnie. I met him in college. We both attended the University of Southern California. But we didn't start dating until after graduation. I was writing Abigail's book and Lonnie was working at a marketing firm. We dated for six months. I'd been up-front with him from the beginning about not wanting anything long-term. He knew all along that I was planning on leaving when my job with Abigail was done, but when the time came, he asked me to marry him instead. I was hurt in so many ways, felt like he'd been lying to me all along in agreeing that we were just enjoying the moment, like I'd been inadvertently forced to hurt someone, when I try so hard not to do that, ever. And I was devastated that he was so hurt. It's something I carry with me, every day. That look on his face when I had to tell him no. I hate, more than anything, that I hurt him."

Her tone was dead serious and Weston knew she was speaking directly to him as she relayed the story.

He reached for her hand, but quickly pulled back before any damage had been done. But he did meet her gaze—in a way that felt deeply personal. "I swear to you, Paige, I'm not Lonnie. I am not misconstruing what's going on here or making it any more than what we've agreed upon. I swear to you. I do not open that door. Ever."

"Ever?" Her question seemed so vulnerable. As though she desperately needed the reassurance.

He shook his head. "I give you my word."

She seemed to need more, hung on to his gaze for some long seconds, and then, with a blink and a smile, said, "Now I believe we should set a statute of limitations on a party bringing up personal conversation after another party has initially introduced the topic."

"Fine."

"The topic is only alive for the duration of the

initial conversation," she stated. "As far as I'm concerned, that's not negotiable."

He had no reason to argue the point with her. "Fine."

"I have evidence to provide to support my argument."

"None necessary."

"I want to present my evidence."

He had to fight back the smile that her doggedness brought to his lips. "I'll hear the evidence."

"I was sitting in a meeting, focused on business, feeling safe in the environment, and it suddenly became an unsafe place for me to be."

He didn't feel like smiling anymore. He felt like a schmuck. "I apologize. Paige, seriously, I'm sorry. I didn't think it through…" Though he'd felt like he'd done nothing but think about it. And while he'd been sidetracked by her story, and felt a little shell-shocked by it for no discernible reason, he still didn't have the information he'd been seeking. "But since we've been on the topic in this conversation, can I ask one more question?"

"I guess."

"When it ended, did you just walk away and never look back?"

"No." That was it. No elaboration.

And he'd used up his one question.

"I don't ever walk away without looking back, West," she said, calling him by the name he'd specifically told her he no longer used. As she did in bed every night. And other times, too, unless she particularly wanted distance.

It was the name she'd come to know him by through his father.

The name of a man she'd said she'd grown to like before she'd even met him.

A name he'd come to adore on her lips. Not that he'd ever admit that aloud.

"I care about the people in my life. I just don't attach to them in a permanent sense."

"I completely get that." And was curiously comforted by what she'd said.

"Lonnie's married now, to a wonderful woman. I like her so much. And they have two kids. Both of whom call me Aunt Paige."

"You still see him?"

"Anytime I'm in Southern California. Which is generally at least once a year, even if just for a long weekend. I love the San Diego beaches. They always soothe something inside me."

She went on about ocean sunsets and wave sounds, while he was still focusing on her being close enough friends with her ex to actually assume a familial role in his life.

He sat back, more relaxed than he'd been in a while. Tried to catch up to ocean breezes, the sounds of crashing waves, blue skies and sunshine.

Happy to listen to her rave about them.

Chapter Seventeen

Paige cried on the day that Darcy left. The tears unraveled her usual zen a bit. Goodbyes didn't make her cry. But Darcy...she'd been the one whose head was on her lap every night the week Walter had died.

She was going to a great home, out in the country, with a ten-year-old boy who needed a companion as badly as Darcy needed to be one, and she was honestly happy for her. Instead of hanging out in a kennel and a pen with her and the other rescues, she'd be running in fields and fishing. Paige had already had a video of the dog in the stream, her head diving below the water for fish, her tail wagging.

Buddy peed on the floor that day, too, and so she took him, alone, with her to walk around the outside of the mansion to check progress on the second kennel and pen. After two weeks of rain, construction was behind, but what had once just been an approved foundation now supported completed framing as well. Letting out several more yards on Buddy's leash, she let him smell and explore to his heart's content, imagining Darcy settling into her new home, scarfing her dinner and sleeping in a bed with her head on a kid's thigh.

And still, peace was elusive. The meeting with West the week before had been some kind of a game changer, but she couldn't say how or why. They'd been together for ten weeks, two and a half of their twelve months, and things couldn't be working out better if she'd been living her best fantasy. The sex was more incredible than any she'd ever heard about or thought possible.

And it was free of entanglement. They were actually making it work, sticking to the boundaries, playing by the rules. She didn't have to carry around unrequited lust. Instead, she got to imagine all of the things she'd like to do with West, knowing that she'd be doing them.

She'd chosen her next work assignment—one she could do long-distance. That was an unusual perk this time around, due to the year she had to spend in Atlanta. She'd be ghostwriting a fantasy novel for a well-known science fiction author and was looking forward to the collaboration as well as to delving into a topic she loved and a type of writing she hadn't done before. All of her stuff to date had been nonfiction.

She had kind of thought it always would be.

But change was good.

And since she couldn't change her venue, she'd changed her genre.

Mariah and Tess had been thrilled when she'd had a video call with them earlier in the day. They really wanted her to branch out and write her own books, rather than letting others take credit for her prose, but they didn't push her. They understood.

Neither of them had been on her back about anything. The entire conversation had been pressure free and she'd loved talking to them.

Life was good. Better than ever.

And she'd cried when Darcy had left.

Sitting on the frame of an outer wall, she leaned her head back against a two-by-four running up to the ceiling frame and tried to figure herself out. Pushing blue feelings away only sent them deeper into her soul, to thrive, reproduce themselves and rise up to bite her when she least expected it.

She had to look at them, sit with them, experience them. But it would help if she understood them.

Deep in self-reflection, she didn't notice at first when Buddy returned from his explorations. Used to him keeping his distance, she'd been content to know he was on a leash and safe and hadn't tried to interact with him as she would have Darcy or some of the others.

She looked back over a lifetime of goodbyes to try to figure out why Darcy's might be affecting her differently, being brutally honest with herself, as she had to be in order to trust herself, and…landed on an answer. In some ways Darcy had been closer to her than the other dogs who'd departed because she'd appointed herself her keeper after Walter's death. She'd managed to climb more deeply into her heart, without her even recognizing that it had been invaded.

And then she'd left. Wagging her tail as she'd been lead away.

She'd left.

Other than those who'd left her through death, which invoked an entirely different type of blue, Darcy was the only one close to her who'd left her.

Usually *she* was the one who left.

The bombshell slammed into her just as she looked up and saw that Buddy had returned. And was sitting upright, watching her, not even a full foot away.

He'd come of his own accord.

Without even questioning whether or not he'd stay put, she reached out a hand to him. "You're a good boy, Bud. The best," she told him. "You know already, huh? And you know I'll make sure you're loved for the rest of your days, too, don't you?"

The dog didn't make a sound. But she counted his eyes half closing in a look of bliss as he sat and let her scratch his chest as his response.

He'd given her his trust.

And she was going to have to ask West to adopt a second dog. It wasn't like they didn't have room.

Buddy would be most comfortable in the kennel permanently, where he could have companionship but not need to interact with human strangers. And with the second kennel coming in a matter of weeks, they'd still be able to take in a lot more animals than Walter had originally planned.

West was already planning to care for fourteen dogs on his own, with possible hired daily help, once Paige left. Whether one of those fourteen was Buddy or someone else wouldn't make a workload difference.

So thinking, she sent him a text to put the topic on the table for their weekly Wednesday-morning meeting two days hence and, shortening Buddy's leash, walked the dog back home.

West noticed a difference in Paige when he had sex with her that night. He'd been waiting for her outside the kennel, with a bottle of wine and some chocolate sauce, because as he'd left her room the night before she'd said she'd like to dip him in chocolate and then, after licking it off him, take a hot bath with him with a glass of wine.

He'd never been a bath guy, but had been dying to get there all day.

She'd been thrilled to see the gifts in his hand and had led him straight upstairs to a room they'd seen on his floor with a huge garden tub, and reality had been far more mind-blowing than any fantasy he'd tried to create.

It was afterward, as they lay, satiated, in a bed of warm bubbles, sipping wine, that she'd seemed to leave him. They were at opposite ends of the double-size tub, her feet alongside him and his toes tracing light lines on her chest now and then.

Her body was there. Her mind was. The rest of her wasn't. Which made no real sense, and yet he totally understood.

He had another surprise for her, one that he was certain she'd love, but put off giving it to her until he knew what was taking her away from her usual sense of peace.

And remembered the text she'd sent earlier in the day.

"Is the dog situation you texted about something we need to discuss before Wednesday's meeting? Something you need an answer to right now?"

Taking a sip of wine, she gave him a slow, sleepy smile that had him growing hard again, but he wasn't going to let his penis control things in spite of the fact that they were all about sex, and no commitment. Didn't mean you had to be inhumane. Or not care.

"No," she said, a few seconds after he'd asked the question. "I'm not worried about the answer. I know what it will be. I just wanted you to know the question was coming." Her seductive smile left no doubt that, while she meant what she said, she was also being sassy with him.

Paige wasn't the sort of person who'd use a guy's weaknesses against him. Or hurt anyone on purpose. She wasn't manipulative and seemed to have no interest in changing anyone's mind about anything, from what he could tell. She just expected to have her own opinions and choices respected as well.

He was all for their mutual respect.

"You're that sure you know what my answer to whatever it is will be?"

"Yep." She licked her lips. And he knew they were going to have sex again before they parted ways that night.

"Am I that much of a pushover?" At the moment he didn't give a damn one way or the other, if she was the one doing the pushing.

"I'd like to roll you over and slide up that body," she said, and the glow in her gaze was all Paige. She'd come back to him.

And, as always, he was happy to accommodate her request.

Though she was still experiencing moments of blueness, Paige was feeling her usual flow of optimistic energy as she pulled on the skirt and top she'd had on when West had commandeered her in the kitchen earlier that evening. The bra and panties that went with them in hand, she was turning to wish him a good night, when he said, "Wait, I have a surprise for you."

Her spirits slowly deflating, she waited.

"No. No, no, no," he said quickly, holding her gaze. "I know you don't like surprises, but this isn't like that," he said. "It's just something I was given today by a software developer who has been wooing me to give him a chance to earn my business. I think you'll actually really enjoy it. I, on the other hand, would never use it."

The needle on her peace-o-meter rose again. "You have a present for me, not a surprise," she said, grinning. "Communication, Thomas. That's the key…"

What an idjit. He'd been being nice and she'd acted like an emotional twit.

On the other hand, if they were going to start giving each other gifts… Her levels of calm started to drop again. What in the hell was the matter with her?

It wasn't a gift specifically for her, she reminded herself quickly. It wasn't like he'd gone out and bought it, or picked it out with her in mind and…

The realization wasn't helping her any.

Standing there in pants only, he grabbed his sport coat off the doorknob and pulled an envelope out of the pocket. Handed it to her.

"It's a trip to the ocean," he told her. "Three days

at an exclusive resort on a private beach. I'm told
one of the best places in Florida…"

She stared at the envelope, freezing up inside.
And didn't move.

Couldn't move.

Why couldn't she move?

Anyone else and she'd take the envelope, thank
them politely, then quietly and safely burn it without opening it as soon as she was alone. There were
a couple of fireplaces in the mansion. And a firepit
outside by the pool, too. She pictured them. Pictured paper burning.

Just as one of her earlier therapists had taught her
to do. If something hurt, she was to write it down
on paper and then slowly and safely destroy it.

Grandma and Tess and Mariah had all suggested
the burning. Because of the whole Mariah, Tess
and Joe thing. There was no Joe in their family, but
that would have been Paige's name if she'd been a
boy. The names came from a song that Mariah and
Tess had been named after, one their parents had
danced to the first night they'd kissed. They were
names for rain and wind and fire. Mariah, in the
song spelled Maria, stood for wind. Tess stood for
rain. And Joe…that was the fire.

Joe, fire, when used safely, could destroy the
memories of what hurt her…a physical ritual to
mimic an emotional letting go. Write down what
hurt you on a piece of paper and watch it burn away.

She could imagine her pain burning down to nothing but ash, letting that gray matter blow away on the wind. Or drown in the rain.

"Paige?"

West's voice came through a fog, and then rang too loud. Bringing her fully back to the present. She tried to mentally hum the tune to the song. To remind herself.

Something she hadn't had to do in more years than she could even recall.

She blinked. Tried to meet West's gaze, but her glance stumbled on the envelope he still held outstretched. Only seconds had passed since his offer.

They felt like years.

"I…um…" She swallowed. "I don't want it," she said. And then, trying hard to get her usual lilt in her voice, added, "But thank you, Weston. It was really sweet of you to offer. I'll bet someone in your office would be thrilled with the gift. Or…maybe Amanda." The woman they dealt with at Operation Rescue.

The stunned expression on his face warned her. She had to go. Say goodbye.

Time to leave.

Her feet seemed stuck to the floor. She couldn't make them move. Instead, she stood there, watching herself as though from a far-off place, knowing that her world was about to disintegrate and she wasn't stopping it from happening.

Her mental resources, her reasoning, her lessons and beliefs, her knowledge and faith and coping mechanisms…they were all there, but limp. Unresponsive.

It was as though everyone who watched over her had vanished and there was only her. All alone. In the dark.

Huddled. Up against warm rubber, shaking, listening and deathly afraid, knowing that she'd be discovered…

"Paige?" West was there.

He wasn't supposed to be there. She didn't know him yet.

His hand on her shoulders was familiar, as was the arm he wrapped around her waist, and so she went with him. Sat on the edge of a bed they'd never used, as she tucked her underwear under her thigh. Hiding it.

She knew where she was. Knew why she was there.

She even knew they'd just had sex in the bath and he'd tried to give her a trip to Florida.

She just didn't know why the pain was there. How it had come back. She hadn't buried it. She'd dealt with it. How could it still exist with enough force to stop her in her tracks?

And what in the hell did she do with it?

"Tell me what's going on." West's voice called her gaze to his. Even there, she saw something she didn't recognize. A look from him that she'd never seen before.

One that didn't belong in her world.

"Are you okay?"

She shook her head a little. Like she might have at eleven, when she'd been a quivering mass of fear and loss. "I don't think so," she said, her voice scratchy in her throat.

"I didn't mean to upset you. You spoke about how much you loved the ocean. Breezes and waves and beaches. When you visit Lonnie. I just… When the guy described the offer he was handing me… I thought it would be perfect for you until you get back across the country…"

Right. Lonnie. Their last business meeting. She'd told West about Lonnie. And San Diego. Lonnie had been the one to get her to the beach. Helping her reframe the idea of going there in her mind by the fact that it was across the country. Or some such thing. It had been a suggestion from a therapist she'd seen in California because her sisters had worried about her out there all by herself.

"I can't go to a Florida resort, West. I don't ever go to Florida."

"Can you tell me why?"

She shook her head. She hadn't even told Lonnie… only what the counselor had said. Until she'd broken up with him and he'd been so devastated. Even then, all she'd done was tell him her real name. Told him to look her up.

He had. And had been a close person in her life ever since.

He was also the last person she'd told.

Her real name. She had to tell West. Just like Lonnie, it was the only way. She opened her mouth, prepared to speak and then break their rules and leave the room. Nothing was the same anymore. Rules weren't going to help…

"I was the only survivor of a brutal carjacking there…"

She heard the words escape, uttered in a tiny, vulnerable voice, and didn't have the strength to get up and go.

Chapter Eighteen

West had no rules to follow. Nothing to guide him. But as soon as he heard Paige's voice, he switched into a gear he didn't know he had. On some level he registered his own shock, but compared to hers, his feelings weren't even on the radar.

He didn't move the arm he'd wrapped around her waist to guide her to the bed, but he didn't pull her closer, either. It was like she was a bomb that was ticking and anything he did or didn't do could cause an explosion.

He wasn't going to let that happen.

No matter what.

Thoughts filled with bravado, perhaps, and yet he didn't doubt their authenticity.

He didn't push, or prod. Had no idea she'd been a victim—ever. Other than the loss of her parents in a car accident as a kid, which had been horrifically tragic in and of itself.

Had no idea when the other event had happened.

He needed to know. But was in complete service to her as long as she needed him to be. As long as she was in the state she was in.

Paige Martinson was the strongest woman, the strongest human being, he'd ever known.

And in the midst of the waiting, of absorbing whatever fraction of her pain that he could, was a flower of thankfulness, too.

She'd survived.

I was the only survivor...

Thank God she'd survived.

"He came out of nowhere." Her tone hadn't changed, not really. She still sounded...like a younger version of herself. "We were stopped at a red light. It was late. I should have been tired, but I was so excited and Grandpa, he was sitting in the front seat with Dad and kept turning around and asking me if I was having fun yet. Mom kept telling him to hush, but I could tell she was excited, too. It was my first trip to Florida and also my first trip where I was the only kid so I didn't have to share."

"Where were your sisters?" The question came naturally to him, though he still had no idea what he was doing.

Or what would be the right thing to do.

There was no right and wrong. Or rather, there'd been such an egregious wrong that there was no right for it. The dread in his gut had hardened into rock.

Because he knew...she'd been a kid...eleven... and her parents hadn't been killed in a car accident. She'd just told him. She was the sole survivor and her mom and dad, who'd died when she was eleven, and a grandfather he'd never heard of, were the people in the car with her.

"Home. Grandma, Mom's mom, was staying with them. They had a cheerleading competition and had begged to be able to do that instead of taking the family trip. Grandpa, my dad's dad, had just lost Grammie, my other grandma, and he and dad were going to be going deep-sea fishing while Mom and I went to the beach. Grandpa paid for the resort and the plane tickets."

Her voice was no stronger, but the words were clearer.

As was the devastation that was going to come. He wanted to put a finger to her lips, to let her know she didn't have to give life to her tale, but the choice wasn't his.

The chance to be there for her was what he'd been given.

"Our plane had landed late and then the rental company messed up, but we finally got a van and were on our way to the resort…"

If she stopped, he'd accept her decision. He wasn't going to ask for any details.

And wondered, was it wrong to hope she'd said all she was going to say? Not for his sake, but for hers?

Why her composure had broken, with him, he had no idea. Surely his offer of a trip to Florida alone wouldn't have done it.

She'd seemed off there for a bit in the tub.

He should have tried harder to find out what had initially upset her.

But their rules…

Just didn't apply.

"He had a gun pointed at my dad's head from outside the car. I was sitting right behind him. I could see it before my mom did, but as soon as she heard the guy order my dad out of the van, Mom shoved me down to the floor. Dad got out. I could feel the weight in the van shift. Mom had me crawl over to her side of the van and she put her legs over me. I heard a gunshot…"

Her father had been executed and she'd been a witness. No way a kid came out of that experience in one piece. But Paige had. She was there.

Telling people's life stories. Loving dogs.

Being kind to Weston even when he'd been a rude, bossy, know-it-all ass.

He hoped they were done with the tale. Didn't know the next steps, what she'd need. Waited for some sign from her.

"I knew what had happened, but Mom was leaning over me. Whispering about how much she and Daddy loved me. That I was always to remember that nothing would ever change that. Ever. And she told me that I had to be very quiet and hide. No matter what. I just had to hide.

"The weight in the van shifted again and the guy's voice… It was right there in the van, next to Grandpa. He told him and Mom to get out. She opened the door, and shoved at me with her foot, so I did what she said and crawled down to the ground so the man couldn't see me. And then crawled under the van to hide. I figured Mom would come get me when it was safe, but then I heard two more gunshots and a loud engine noise and a screech, and horrible-smelling smoke went up my nose. I was afraid I was going to cough or sneeze, but then the van was gone and I was laying there flat in the middle of the road. I was afraid to move. But I looked over, and that's when I saw Mom. She was on the ground with her mouth open and liquid dripping out."

West had known pain in his life. He couldn't remember his mother's death, but he knew the pain of growing up without her. And the grief of losing Mary...

Nothing compared to what Paige had suffered... there was no way anything could...

"I guess I moved off the road. Next thing I remember, I was huddled in some trees, freezing and shaking, still hiding, and there were sirens and lights swirling and shining, too, all over, and lots of people, and someone found me and then hollered, 'I've got her! She's over here!'"

Again, gratitude swept through him. She'd been found! He wanted to pull her onto his lap, wrap his arms around her and cuddle her close for however long it took to help her feel warm and loved again.

Because he knew, as sure as he was sitting there, why Paige Martinson didn't do relationships. Why she shied away from the security and comfort and love and sharing brought about by long-term commitments. Her belief in all of that had been wiped away with three rapid gunshots.

The bullets might not have hit her, but he knew as clearly as if he'd read her mind that those bullets had wrapped her sweet young self in a wall of steel that no human being would ever be able to penetrate.

How could she remember so clearly? Sitting there on an unused bed, with West's arm loosely at her back, Paige shook inside, continuing to exist in unfamiliar territory. She knew where she was. Who she was with. She knew why she was there. She could remember the day clearly.

She just didn't recognize her inner self. It was as though something had broken and an entire flood of existence was surging forth. She didn't remember ever having such acute memories of the night her parents and grandfather had been killed.

"I can see their faces," she said aloud. Her mother's mouth…she had no recollection of ever having seen that before and yet she'd described it in such detail to West. She must have seen it to have the image in her brain. "From under the van I can see all three of them. Dad on one side, Mom and

Grandpa on the other. There's a streetlight. It's like being on a stage. And when the van roars away, I'm left there. I have to hide."

She had to hide.

Looking up at West, she saw him clearly. "Mom told me to hide and that's all I knew. Obviously, I was in shock," she said. "I ran off for a distance, until I found some shrubbery to push myself into. Then I just stayed there. I've... I think this is the first time I'm remembering all this," she admitted to him. Feeling weak. And stupid.

"I'm not all that up on the inner workings of the human mind." West's voice sounded real, solid, so she listened as he continued, "But I saw a documentary once about the effects of trauma on the psyche and it basically said that our minds have tremendous inner protective systems. They hide things from us if they're above our emotional capacity, and then show them to us when we have the emotional capacity to cope with them."

Another memory surfaced. "I had a counselor tell me something like that once. But at that point, I'd already remembered the key stuff. I didn't realize there was more buried there."

Nor did she know the ramifications of it coming forth.

Was there more yet to come? Did she finally have it all out?

And why then? Why that night?

Why had she cried when Darcy left?

What was happening inside her? Wrong with her?

"I'll call my last therapist in the morning," she said aloud. "I haven't spoken to her in several years, but I get emails from her office every now and then, just checking in."

"I've never heard of a therapist keeping in contact with patients years after they'd stopped seeing them."

She shrugged, not wanting to lose what she'd recovered of her little girl self, but not wanting to dwell there, either. That look on her mother's face… it was going to haunt her for the rest of her life.

Had it always been haunting her and she just hadn't known it? What did it mean, now that she was consciously seeing it?

She'd always been so honest with herself. And now she was finding out that, in essence, she'd been lying to herself all along?

And what did West have to do with it all? Surely she hadn't just needed an offer of a Florida getaway to unlock the vault inside her.

Or maybe it was just that simple. A straw-that-broke-the-camel's-back kind of thing.

"Where is she located?"

His question confused her at first. She felt lost for a second.

The therapist. They'd been talking about her therapist. He found it odd that she kept in touch.

His impression was valid.

"She's in California. And in most cases, therapists probably can't keep in touch with every client that passes through their careers." It was time to come out.

Maybe with just West.

Maybe with others. She didn't even want to contemplate what that might mean. For her. For her sisters. Their husbands. Their lives.

It was too much. She shook her head.

"I have something to tell you, but I need you to swear to me, West, that you won't repeat it to anyone, not even aloud to yourself until I can figure this out more."

"You have my word." And it came immediately. In a nonnegotiable tone. She could trust him.

"My real name is Paige Anders."

She felt him flinch. Didn't blame him. And felt an immediate chill through her body as he removed his arm from around her.

He didn't move away, though. He was right there. "You aren't Paige Martinson?" It was almost as though she could feel his brain churning out thoughts, she felt that connected to him.

"I am Paige Martinson," she assured him. "Legally and completely. Everything you find about her on the internet is me. And if you pull out your phone and search for Paige Anders, you're going to understand a whole lot more."

She waited. It was just easier that way. She'd been through it with Lonnie and had promised herself that that would be the last time.

She wasn't in the habit of breaking her own promises. Didn't like that it had just happened.

And just wanted the job done, whatever that might turn out to mean.

What came after, she had no idea. There was no great need to get up and go. But she knew she wouldn't stay, either. Not past the year she'd promised West.

And maybe their sexual fling was done.

He'd pulled out his phone as she'd suggested. He'd be reading about the incredibly brave little girl who'd witnessed her family's horrendous murders and had had the strength to save herself. How it was a miracle the wheels of that van hadn't rolled right over her. How she'd have been dead for sure if the carjacker had known she was there. He'd be reading about how she'd insisted on talking to the police. And, after the arrest, had been distraught until her grandmother had taken her down to Florida to sit in court, face him down and testify that yes, she recognized his voice. And his face, from her position on the floor when he'd turned around to look at her mother. How, in a clear though trembling voice, she'd told the court what that man had done to her family that night.

About how she'd made national news and the condolences, the support, waves of sympathy and donations had deluged her after that. There'd been talk of a TV movie. Enough money to pay for her college and then some. Documentaries had been made.

"You testified."

Yep. He'd gotten there.

"I can't believe anyone would let a little girl go through that."

"I didn't give them much choice." She had no trouble remembering those parts. "I went on a hunger strike. Just refused to eat. They even put me on an IV for a short period of time. In the end, my therapist believed me when I kept telling her that the only way I could be okay was if I could make the man go away forever."

"You had to take control of making him pay for what he'd done."

She stared at him. He totally got it. Lonnie had gone on and on about how her loved ones should have found a way to help her see that it wasn't in her best interests to testify. That they'd known better than a then prepubescent, nearly twelve-year-old girl.

She wanted West's arm back around her. Only

for a moment or two. She was exhausted. Mentally, physically, but mostly emotionally.

More than she could ever remember being.

"And the press hounded you, after that."

"I couldn't walk out my door without someone wanting to see how I was doing. To just get a quote. I couldn't go to school. The kids were all over me. We moved, but that didn't help. It didn't take long for people to find us. It was bad for my sisters, too. They were in high school and were followed everywhere. Eventually our family attorney, after talking to my therapist I think, suggested a name change."

"How many people in your current life know about this?"

"My sisters, their husbands and Lonnie. And my therapist."

"My father didn't know."

"No."

But now West did. His name on that list was telling.

She just didn't know what it was saying.

And didn't want him jumping to conclusions, either.

"I'm sorry you had to witness my breakdown," she told him, forcing herself to stand. "No way you deserved to have that all laid on you. It's not what we signed up for. And as to the rest, please, other than keeping it to yourself, just forget it. I'm not Paige Anders anymore. I haven't been for a long time. I'm Paige Martinson and I'm happy with the life I've made for myself."

He stood too, was only inches from touching her front to front, was frowning. "You're Paige Anders, too," he said softly. "I'm no therapist, but it's pretty clear that she's a part of you that's looking for some kind of voice."

Maybe. That was for her to figure out. Possibly with Christine's help. She'd be calling the therapist as soon as her office opened in the morning. With the time difference that meant she had to hold on until 11:00 a.m.

She had a lot to process in the meantime.

"And while I appreciate your apology, I can't accept it as I don't believe it's called for," West continued on after a short pause. He had her attention, in a peripheral way. "In my opinion, you didn't break down. You had a breakthrough. I don't know why it happened now, but I know that I'm glad I was here. Tonight is something I will always remember. And I will always be glad I was the one to share it with you."

She remained in the room with him but gave him what she had. Silence.

He didn't leave, either. Maybe it wasn't time. Maybe they weren't done. She didn't know. She just didn't go.

"What can I do to help? What do you need from me?"

Finally, a question for which she had a clear response. "Can we just continue on with our plan?" Her calm tone had returned. She recognized it with gratitude. "Other than my…episode…and your knowing about my past, nothing has changed. The present is still what it was. Our choices are what they are."

And she was standing there with a bra and pair of panties in her hand. Too tired. In need of being supine and unconscious for a bit.

"Of course." Again, he answered immediately. "Just know that I'm here if you need to talk. If you need anything."

She nodded. What she didn't need was any more sympathy. Not in her current lifetime. Though she knew, rationally, that it was given in caring, it made her feel like a victim. It weakened her.

"I just need you to treat me as you always have, West."

He nodded.

"Unless…this changes things for you? Is this the point where we end our sexual partnership?" She was fairly sure she didn't want him to, but at the moment, as numb as she was, the time was good for him to tell her if he was finished.

"I'm nowhere near done." Another definitive answer. One that brought a surge of feeling back to her. She teared up. Turned to the door.

And when she'd blinked her gaze clear, looked at

him over her shoulder. He was still standing, bare-chested, right where she'd left him. Watching her.

"I'm not done, either, West," she said, just in case there'd been any doubt about that. "Sleep well."

She hoped he would. He was a good man. A good business partner. A good lover.

And whether they'd planned it or not, he'd become a good friend.

Chapter Nineteen

It took everything Weston had to get up and go to work the next morning as though nothing had changed.

After all, she'd asked to be treated as though nothing had changed. He'd given his word he'd do so. Just, in the cold light of day, he had no idea how to go about doing that.

The battle inside him had raged as he'd showered and shaved, pressed his gray dress slacks with the board and iron in his closet, knotted the gray-and-white geometric-design tie atop his white shirt. Did he check on her?

Or just head out the door as usual?

Did he make an excuse for needing to see her?

The idea was a compromise, but he hadn't been able to come up with a legitimate excuse. Paige was smart. She'd have seen through the subterfuge, and then he'd lose at least a modicum of her trust.

It was Paige's morning to tend to the dogs and he did venture into the laundry room before walking out the door, just to make sure she hadn't overslept. As soon as he heard her voice crooning to the animals, he quickly backtracked before someone noticed him.

He'd spent the night tossing and turning, dozing, dreaming about her and waking to think about her in the darkness. Wondering if she was asleep. If she was suffering.

Thinking about the incredible young girl who'd managed to keep herself alive, and then testify against her family's killer.

And wondering if his dad had figured out her secret. There'd been a reason Walter had named her as co-owner of the estate.

He wondered what his father would have him do now that he knew.

How could he help Walter's last great idea come to fruition? What did Paige need from him?

He had questions and no answers.

Was his job to know about her past and treat her no differently? Was that what she needed?

Her struggle wasn't about him. Maybe it was just coincidence that she'd had a major moment while in his presence. Could be that it hadn't had anything to do with him at all.

The one thing he didn't question was how much he cared. About her. About what she'd been through. About her. About her future. About her.

That was the sum total of his clarity. He cared for Paige Martinson. He wouldn't say he was in love with her. But he cared.

As she'd said, nothing had changed. Not for her, but not for him, either. He didn't want forever any more than she did. For different reasons, but the end result was the same.

And yet, he couldn't deny the intensity of emotion that she raised in him. Sexually it was beyond even being close to anything he'd ever known.

He'd never known anything like his connection to her in other ways, too. The way she drew him to her with just a look. Held him there just by breathing.

Maybe she felt some of the same. Maybe that was why she'd had her breakthrough with him. Because some part of her had recognized that he was safe.

He liked that idea. Hoped he was right.

Didn't figure he was ever going to know one way or the other.

She texted him while he was eating takeout Chinese food from a carton in his office during a brief lunch break.

Spoke to my therapist in California. Apparently last night was the godsend she and my sisters have been waiting for all these years. Everything is well. And lesson to self: don't ever get so smug that you think you know it all.

He was just starting to type a response when the brief missive was followed a few seconds later with: Thanks for sitting through it with me.

Erasing his first partial message, something that was supposed to have sounded as kind but distant as her original text but hadn't succeeded, he typed, You're welcome. Read it twice. And hit Send.

Anything else he might have expressed either wasn't within the boundaries marked by their rules, or it had already been said.

He put his phone down, tucked in the four cardboard flaps of the lid to his lunch, tossed the cheap wooden chopsticks in the trash, and was collecting a couple of folders to take down the hall with him to a meeting with his small staff when his phone binged again.

You up for skinny-dipping in our temporarily jointly owned pool tonight?

I'm up just thinking about it, he typed back. And with a smile on his face, went to work.

Yeah, in some ways it would be hard watching Paige go at the end of the year.

Life wasn't perfect.

But, as Paige had said a few times, it had perfect moments.

And he was glad.

A week passed and while her days moseyed along with normal activities, as regularly scheduled, Paige experienced them differently. As someone different.

And yet the same, too.

Life with West was as great, as always. The sex was still as inventive and thrilling and just plain… sexy. She still saw stars when she exploded with repletion.

She still slept alone.

And she felt a new absence when she was with him, too. A lack that hadn't been there before. As though he was pulling away from her. She'd known it was going to happen eventually. Would have liked for it to happen mutually, and closer to the year's end, but she also accepted that that particular choice was out of her control. What she could do, and did do, was choose to continue to enjoy every intimate moment she had with him as long as she had them.

She'd started work on her new project. Loved the plot outline the author had sent to her. The character descriptions. And was enjoying getting lost in the prose flying from her fingers. She'd done some initial writing up in her study, but since her memory eruption, she'd started taking her laptop to the kennel more often than not.

At their business meeting two days after her meltdown, West had agreed to adopt Buddy, and she was trying to maintain the progress they'd made with the dog. He still wouldn't come all the way up to them when called, but he got within an arm's reach of either one of them. And sat long enough to have the little piece of white fur on his chest get a rub or two.

Paige felt better keeping an eye on little Angel, who, while gaining weight, was showing no improvement at all in terms of fatigue and overall behavior. It was like her puppy body had been given an old spirit. Sometimes Angel liked Paige to pet her and would snuggle up on the couch with Paige and Annie. And other times, she strained to be away and would end up alone in a bed in the corner of the room. At no time did she show any playful puppy behavior. And her potty training was hit-or-miss as well.

Sometimes, Paige felt an affinity with Angel that many probably wouldn't understand. Like they were both ancient entities trapped in younger lives.

Even as she entertained the thought, she recognized the fancy in her thinking and the fatigue in her heart. Christine had assured her the exhaustion would pass.

And that it was absolutely normal, too, considering her recent emotional outburst. So like her not to reveal her trauma in spurts. No, she'd just blow it all out there at once.

She was in almost daily contact with the counselor that week, not because she had anything new to say, or was struggling to the point of needing Christine, but as a grounding place, a check-in to know for sure that she didn't need further help.

Her therapist had assured Paige that her brain had done its job well, holding back until she was fully ready, and then trusting her to handle the rest. Christine said that self-reflection had become a part of Paige's daily life since the Lonnie episode, and Paige had made it a big part of her current mental and emotional well-being.

It was all good to know.

And in some ways, didn't help at all.

She couldn't get the sight of her mother's face out of her mind. But she didn't want to forget. No more hiding bombshells from herself just to have them reappear without her calling for them. But she had to be able to get through days without that jolt of shock in her stomach when the vision came to her.

It wasn't just that one image, of course. There were others. Her dad. Her grandpa. The dirty undercarriage of the van. Tires moving so close to her body that they ran over her hair. She knew, even without Christine having told her multiple times, that learning to live with these newly resurfaced memories would just take time. Her conscious brain was in the process of accepting them. Once they'd been fully admitted, Paige would be able to file them away.

She needed to talk to her sisters. Christine asked a couple times over that week if she'd called them yet. But when she'd explained that she was feeling pretty strongly that she wanted to have the conversation in person, Christine had acknowledged that the idea might be a good one. And she'd agreed that it might be better if Paige waited until she'd had more time to process, to be more comfortable with the added information before trying to share it with anyone who would also have a vested interest in it.

The therapist had just been eager for Paige to have access to the comfort she thought Mariah and Tess would bring her.

Paige wasn't so sure they would, though. Her sisters both lived with their own guilt and struggles where the carjacking was concerned. They were supposed to have been there. Took responsibility for the little sister who'd had to get through the horrific tragedy all alone.

Of course, she'd told them, multiple times, that if they'd been there, they likely would have been killed, too, and then they wouldn't have been alive and waiting for her to come home to.

But Tess and Mariah also needed to know what happened to their family. They craved details, to be able to share those last minutes, as though by doing so, they could properly say goodbye. They'd never told Paige directly, but their gentle probing over the years had given her that understanding.

She also acknowledged that she could possibly have it all wrong where they were concerned. The mental uncertainty was new to her and she wasn't feeling even a little bit cordial toward it.

Darcy had been gone a week and they still didn't

have a foster replacement. She was feeling the lack, even while she acknowledged that, with her own spiral, and Angel's struggles, it might not have been fair to bring a new needy being into the mix.

At lunchtime that Tuesday, one week after her life had changed so drastically and yet not at all, she took Buddy on a walk over to see how the construction was progressing. She liked to go during lunch break so the workers wouldn't be there, or at least would be congregating over at their trucks. She didn't want to push Buddy back into his shell.

As had become a bit of a habit, she took a picture of the cocker mix nosing around walls that were partially sheet-rocked and texted it to West.

Also, as usual, he sent back a thumbs-up emoji. It came in just as she was taking Buddy's leash off back inside the kennel. She saw it, but didn't send back her usual smiley face as a sudden mewling cry sent fear tearing through her. Setting her phone on the counter by the outside door, she started doing a head count. Looking everywhere for the source of the sound. It was in the room. Sounded close. Annie, Abe and Checkers were all three at the door, greeting her, hoping for treats, she was sure.

Which only left Angel, and the little girl was nowhere to be seen. Another sharp, high almost growling sound rent the air and Paige's panic intensified. She grabbed her phone—remembered 911 was only for humans—and bent to peer under first one couch then the other, looking around cup-boards, into corners, behind dog beds.

And noticed Checkers nudging his big nose up under the twin bed she and West had brought down from upstairs.

Another clearly pained half yelp, half growl sounded and Paige ran, landed roughly on her knees and bent, her long skirt tangling in her flip-flops, as she peered into the darkness. She saw a shadow, but couldn't see what could possibly be trapping the little dog.

Unless…had she gone there to die?

Fumbling with her phone, she got the flashlight function activated and pointed the beam toward the far corner.

She saw the blood first. What appeared to be a lot of it. In a puddle. And then she noticed another little movement. A mouse maybe?

Had the sick pup been bitten by one? Was the rodent rabid?

Before she could find enough sense to call some-one, she saw another little movement. And it hit her. Their puppy hadn't been sick.

She'd been pregnant! A baby having babies.

Once she knew what she was dealing with, Paige was all business. Careful not to disturb Angel too much, she moved the bed just enough to have good access to the mama and her newborns. Two of them, she could see that clearly. Angel had already licked the placenta membrane away and chewed off the umbilical cord. Both puppies were breathing.

Thank God Angel had had such a small litter.

Not wanting to let them out of her sight, she did so only long enough to get the others outside, closing off the doggy door, and then grabbing some towels and fresh bowls of water.

Angel had already done the work. Paige just wanted to clean them new babies off and make sure no one needed emergency vet service.

Another horrible howl had Paige rushing back over to the far side of the room, a sick feeling in her stomach.

Angel wasn't done yet.

And mamas often needed more time than Angel could possibly have taken to rest between deliveries. But another puppy was clearly on the way.

It seemed to be happening way too fast.

Over the next couple hours, Paige did what she could to help the little girl birth two more pups. A total of four. She soothed Angel as she could. Praised her. Gave her space. Her phone had rung once, clearly upsetting Angel, who jumped at the sound, so Paige turned down the volume. It was Christine, who'd checked in each afternoon. She couldn't deal with a therapist right then. Her own problems didn't figure into this event.

A few minutes after the fourth pup was out and Mama had licked her clean, Angel seemed to finally relax. The dog was exhausted, her head almost on the ground as she surveyed her offspring. All four were golden, like their mama, two male and two female. Curled up next to Angel, they were squirming some, pushing into each other. No eyes had opened yet.

Just as Paige was getting ready to call Amanda at Operation Rescue to report the birth, and to see if she and West could keep the pups—in which case she would ask a vet to make a house call, just in case—or if Amanda would want to send someone to collect them all, Angel whimpered.

And then howled again, a weaker, sickly-sounding cry, and a couple of minutes later, Paige saw why. The poor thing had a fifth pup coming, but it was breech. Angel could still pull the pup out if she had the energy to do so.

All could be well.

But the dog just licked at her opening and howled.

If Paige didn't do something, she was probably going to lose both of them.

She'd watched a normal puppy birth online shortly after she'd come to work for Walter, when she'd given herself a crash course in raising abused dogs, but knew nothing about assisting. Angel whimpered and Paige knew she didn't have time to call anyone.

Going on instinct, she saw the problem, reached

as gently as she could with one finger, hoping she'd figure out what to do to help. She knew the goal. Problem was, she didn't know how best to get the pup out safely. Did she try to turn it completely around? Guide it out? Should she pull at it?

She couldn't let them die.

If she moved wrong, she could kill them.

She couldn't be a direct witness to any more death. She was the only one there, just like before, and this time she'd find a way to keep those with her alive.

She heard steps in the laundry room just as West's voice boomed out a worried-sounding "Paige?"

"Right here," she called, not aware until then that she was on the verge of tears. She couldn't cry. She had to see what she was doing.

"You didn't send back a smile response, and then didn't answer my calls…" His words broke off as he came to an abrupt halt and took in the scene.

"It's breech," she said, afraid to pull her finger out, but afraid to move it, too. "I have no idea what I'm doing."

"I do," he told her, kneeling down on the messy floor in his pristine work clothes to gently stroke Angel's head, telling the dog it would be okay.

And then he started instructing Paige. Telling her how to loop her finger around one leg and then another, gently easing them out. Mentioning that he and Walter had birthed puppies for a neighbor once. And his simple words gave her the confidence to assist the young mama. While he coached, and did what he could to comfort Angel, she did what he told her to do to save the animals.

Five minutes after he arrived, the fifth puppy was birthed and placenta was licked away by a very tired Angel. She was clearly exhausted, her young body limp, but there was no sign of hemorrhaging. And all five babies had steady heartbeats, strong enough to be obvious to the touch of West's and Paige's fingers, and were already looking for full teats. Angel hadn't come into her milk, and yet she moved her tired body to accommodate the pups and all five of them squirmed up to her warmth and began to suckle.

West started cleaning up around them.

Feeling the threat of tears again, Paige stood and made her way over to the sink. Washed her hands. Saw the blood smears on her white shirt, noticed how they blended in with the red and white cotton of her skirt, and went to get her phone. To call Amanda.

And when the woman said a vet would be coming to collect Mama and babies, she sat with West, watching the young family alternately eat and sleep, talking about what had just happened. Paige gave him a blow-by-blow account from the time she'd come in with Buddy, and he let her know that when he hadn't been able to reach her, he'd panicked and driven home. They spoke softly, just a presence with Angel, letting her know that she wasn't alone. And they pet the pups so the babies would be used to human touch.

Neither mentioned showering, changing, or anything outside of the experience they'd just shared.

The vet arrived with a whelping bed carrier and West helped her transport the new family out to her van.

That's when Paige started to cry again.

She'd done it.

She'd faced another death on her watch, and that time she'd won.

For a second there, she could feel the heat of a thousand suns embracing her.

The smiles of her parents, telling her "job well done."

And she let the tears flow.

Chapter Twenty

West returned to the kennel to find Paige gone without a word to him. He knew that it wasn't a good sign. But per their rules, he didn't go after her. She'd disappeared upstairs to her quarters. He could hear her moving around up there from the foot of her staircase.

Needing a shower, he headed up to his own suite, let the hot spray relax him a bit, toweled off and pulled on a pair of dark blue lounging pants and a T-shirt. He normally only wore the attire when he was home alone, but after walking through the house naked with Paige, there didn't seem much point in any kind of formality between them.

He'd been worried about her all week. She'd been as good as her word, returning to life as normal, including the incredible sex, and yet, after what she'd been through, what they'd shared the night of her breakthrough, he couldn't help finding all of the normalcy a bit unnatural.

The other side of that story could be that she was dealing with the fallout on her own, and he just wasn't invited to be privy to it. He knew she was talking to her therapist. She'd offered up a casual comment on Friday that Christine had said that afternoon that she wished she lived closer and could adopt Abe.

The second scenario, that he just wasn't being included in the recovery, was much more likely than Paige trying to pretend that nothing had happened.

She was perfectly fine handling her affairs without him.

And still, he'd worried.

Almost to the point of wishing their year was up and she could just go. That he could get it over with.

And yet, when he'd been unable to reach her that afternoon, the fear that had pierced him had been irrepressible. He'd felt it once before. The day he'd gotten the call that Mary had taken a turn for the worse and if he wanted to see her, he'd better get to the hospital as soon as possible.

Paige not answering the phone didn't even begin to compare to his fiancée on her deathbed. He knew that.

Was gravely disturbed by the way he'd been driven to leave work and get home as soon as possible.

And had only been slightly vindicated to find out that Paige had needed him right then. That his rash action might have saved a puppy's life. And Angel's, too.

Fear for the dogs wasn't what had propelled him home.

He kept to their agreement, left her alone until feeding time. She had the shift solo, but when he joined her in the kennel room it was almost as though she'd been waiting for him. Wordlessly, she handed him a couple of filled bowls—Checkers's and Abe's—and he put them down in their respective places along the wall.

They took care of the dogs with no conversation between them, speaking only to the animals. But when they were done, instead of heading toward the door, as Paige normally did when they shared feeding time, she sat down in the middle of her favorite couch. The one Darcy had always shared with her.

She hadn't asked him to stay. There was no way he was leaving her like that, though.

He sat down. She'd put on some kind of lounge pants, too, silky and loose fitting, except at the waist where the short T-shirt she'd worn with them kept showing a bit of the smooth, tanned skin where her waist met her ribs.

He'd kissed every inch of her skin.

He didn't want to say goodbye.

Not that night. Not any night.

Not ever.

But he didn't want to risk forever, either. Not any more than she did.

Nor could he lose his father's house.

"I'm a mess, West." That name. The one he'd gone by when he'd been carefree and always looking forward to the next great adventure, just like Walter.

"How so?" he asked, just needing to hear her out. To understand. Even if it meant that they were done.

She shook her head and there were tears in her eyes as she looked at him. "This is at least the third time I've cried this week. And I don't ever cry."

That one was a no-brainer. "You had intense emotion bottled up inside you for an exceptionally long time. I'm surprised you aren't in constant tears."

She nodded. Looked toward Annie, who was in Angel's pen with a bowl of food, taking at least a third bite. "I'm sure I'm emotional because of *that*," she allowed. "Obviously, I am. But…it's more than that. Or rather, in addition to it." She was frowning and he knew something big was coming.

And that it had to do with him.

She was going to leave. Soon.

Before the year was up. Giving up all rights to the estate, and all access to the dogs, too, if he abided by the will's stipulations.

Which he had to do or he'd lose the house.

"Darcy leaving…the sadness was so much more acute than my goodbyes ever are. And Angel and babies going, right after we saved them…same thing."

"It sounds like you've been emotionally woken up." He had no idea if that was right. But it was logical.

"I made a soul promise to your dad. It's something I didn't think I could ever break. How can I meet them all again with open arms if I've broken a promise to them?"

Her awaiting tribe, again. He didn't know how to help with that.

So he went with the mundane. "You're thinking of breaking the promise?" Because of him?

She shrugged. Shook her head.

And the relief that flooded him made him feel drunk there for a second.

"I don't know what I'm thinking," she said. And then, looking him right in the eye, said, "Maybe."

He wasn't so happy then. And yet, he wasn't arguing, either.

"Your dad wanted me to own this house because he said ownership would teach me something vital. His last invention, this…project…for the two of us. For me, at least, it had to do with helping me grow, gaining some knowledge that ownership would give me. He hoped that newfound knowledge would bring me more happiness."

West heard her words, and sat there, stunned. Cool and hot all at once. And filled with a clarity so bright he was almost blinded by it. Internally. There was nothing else there.

"I have no idea what he specifically wanted me to get from that, though," she admitted. "I don't know what he meant. And I don't know if I can stick around long enough to find out. But I can't let myself break the promise, either. It's like I'm trapped in this vortex and…"

She saw West's nod, or must have seen something in his expression, because she stopped midsentence and said, "What?"

"I get it now," he said. "I get his last project."

She turned, one leg curled up on the couch, knee to him, the other foot on the floor. "Then can you please fill me in?"

"My dad always said that the way to more happiness was to live each moment as if it was the last, living it fully, enjoying it completely, with a contingency plan that would lead to more happiness if you were still present when that moment ended."

She was listening, seeming to need more information, and so he just started talking as thoughts came to him. "That's what he wanted for us both. The contingency plan. We each thought we were happy, but we were floating on the surface of life, not living it deeply. Living deeply, *that's* the contingency plan. I always thought he had a new and different one for each circumstance. You know, the next invention, that was the contingency.

"But that wasn't it. The contingency plan was love. Love is what brings you happiness and even if you lose it in one moment, you will only be happy if you let your heart find it in the next moment, too." He knew he was right. It felt like his father was speaking to him from the grave. Or more like Walter had been speaking to him his entire life and he was only just then listening. Hearing him. He thought of the room upstairs on his dad's wing. A room he hadn't yet been back inside. The one with all the photos. "And sometimes, the love that makes you happy in the moment isn't with a person who's sharing your space. It can be a love from the past, and while the person might be gone, the love lives on. Remembering it brings happiness."

He sounded like some kind of mental health professional. Walter probably should have been one.

Paige's gaze hadn't left his. He was holding on to her, too. If he let go, his entire life was going to obliterate, and he didn't know what he'd be left with.

"I don't think Dad was planning for us to fall in love. But he knew that you'd lost your parents young and that you were a loner. Just as he knew that I was. I also lost my mother young. And then Mary. His idea was to put two lost, hurting souls together in the hopes that we'd see ourselves in each other. Or, at the very least, understand each other, and in so doing, provide a companionship that might help us each find our way out."

He hadn't written his father's memoirs, or heard all the recorded conversations but he knew Walter Thomas and he knew he was right.

"Dad didn't force us to marry because he didn't know if we'd fall in love and a loveless marriage is the total opposite of what he wanted us to find. With each other, or anyone else. He just hoped we'd become friends."

It all made sense. His dad had never been one to force anyone to do anything, which was why the will had been so confusing all along.

And yet, Walter had spent his entire life trying to find ways to fill voids that would help people live happier lives. To invent objects that made things easier.

And to be an example of finding happiness after disappointment. After grief.

After death.

He had no idea where this understanding left him.

But it made him very thankful and proud that Walter Thomas had been his dad.

How was ownership of the place where she lived supposed to teach her about love? She knew how to love. She did love. Her sisters, who were still on the earth. Lonnie. Darcy and Erin and all of the other dogs she and Walter had cared for and said goodbye to. She still loved her parents and her grandparents. Walter.

And Walter's son.

She loved West.

But that didn't change her need to wander. Love went with her.

But she could see how West had needed the revelation.

"I feel like we've definitely become friends," she finally offered into the silence. She didn't want him to leave her there. Didn't want the conversation to stop yet. And had no idea where it needed to go.

"You've become more than a friend to me." He sounded pained, not happy as the words broke from him. "I'm probably so deeply in love with you I'll never get out."

He sounded…so calm. And like he was speaking through a dry throat, too.

She computed the words. Didn't feel particularly shocked. Or alarmed, either. Shouldn't she have? She wasn't allowed to feel anything in the being in love department. "I might be that far gone, too," she said, when her insides started to tremble. "But you're a black-and-white kind of guy who stays put, and I have a wandering soul."

He hadn't refuted her point. Oh, God, he wasn't shaking his head, telling her she was wrong.

They were different people who needed different things.

Her truth held her steady.

"So where does this all leave us?"

He'd just told her he was deeply in love with her. West was in love with her?

While her heart palpitated, and a part of her

wanted to launch herself into his arms, she couldn't let herself be blinded by what couldn't be.

She. Just. Couldn't.

"Let's talk as friends," he suggested. Their gazes were still locked. She'd never have thought two people could look at each other continuously for so long. Even in their silence, they didn't break eye contact.

She was lost. Couldn't find the person she knew herself to be. And didn't know how to take a step without her.

"What's getting in the way of your happiness?" West asked, as though they were actually just going to sit there and keep talking. "What would make you happy? And…did you just tell me that you're in love with me?"

She nodded. She had to. Truth was her moniker. "But that's not a good thing."

Good. There. Words. Out loud.

His expression changed. Closed a bit. But when he should have ended the conversation, he just repeated, "What would make you happy, Paige?"

She couldn't leave. They had the rule. No walking out. And it hit her, the only way she was going to get out of that moment and into the next was to answer his question. "That's just it, West, I've always thought I was happy."

He nodded. "Because you know where you're headed. You live for the love that waits for you when you get there. Living for the more perfect love because it doesn't end in death. And you love on earth with the goodbye already in mind…"

He understood. Her chest lightened. Breath came easier.

"But what if…what if there's more happiness here in this life, too? You aren't afraid of death, but what if a different fear is holding you back in the present? Preventing a more perfect happiness on earth?"

She didn't think so. Shook her head.

His gaze intensified. She wanted to break away. The tie binding them wouldn't let her, though.

Her eyes felt strained. Moisture came to soothe them. Not enough to be tears. Not enough to spill over.

"What if you're afraid of counting on someone to be here for you, afraid of needing them here, and having them be snatched away in an instant, with no warning, no time to prepare, and no ability to prevent it from happening?"

"That's…" Finally, she'd broken free, could look away. "Ridiculous," she finished with more strength than she'd felt in a while.

"Is it?"

She glanced at him and then quickly moved her gaze on, wouldn't let herself get sucked in again. "Of course."

"You just admitted you love me."

Yeah, she loved her sisters, too. And the dogs. She loved Lonnie.

West was deeply in love with her, though. And she felt the same way.

And suddenly she was pissed. Staring straight at him, she asked, "What are *you* afraid of, West?"

And what in the hell did home ownership have to do with any of it?

"The women I love dying."

His words struck a chord of understanding within her. "That's ridiculous," she said again, albeit less forcefully.

"Yeah." He nodded, his gaze almost compassionate now, as she looked at her. "But it resonated with me so deeply that today, when I couldn't get you on the phone, I walked out on an afternoon of meetings to get home and make sure you were okay."

She loved him for that. So much.

Home. He'd come home to find her. Because home was where your love was stored.

A vision of Walter's picture room upstairs came to her. The old man hadn't lived in the past. But when he'd been near the end of his life, he'd been happy with the love he'd known.

And he'd been loving West, and Paige some, too.

West was deeply in love with her.

She was in love with him, too.

"Home is where your love is stored," she said aloud. Feeling tired. So tired.

And, suddenly, strangely alive.

"Home is what I've been running from." Her

eyes filled with tears for real. They welled up, spilled over and then started pouring. "Oh my God, West, home is what scares me."

She sniffed. Wiped at the tears. But couldn't stop them from falling. Darcy's leaving…it had changed "home" for her. A home she hadn't known had grown on her.

"Home scares me," she said again, looking herself honestly in the face.

"Me, too," West told her, sounding much more calm than she felt. "I've chosen to live alone without fear, rather than love another woman and risk having her vacate our home."

Her tears slowed, her hands dropping to her lap. She held on to his gaze, though.

"But you love me deeply."

"I do." He didn't play chicken like she had. He didn't look away.

"And I love you, too."

He nodded.

"We already have joint ownership of a house."

"I know."

Tension built within her. A thin thread.

Of steel.

Did she have the strength to break it?

Would she rather become a coward and leave? Be untrue to what her heart was telling her?

Self-honesty was her rock. The one thing she knew she could count on.

The one thing she'd promised herself she'd take when she left life and rejoined her tribe. The one thing she'd always known would make her parents proud of her.

"Would you be opposed to me staying on indefinitely after my year is up? I'd still sign ownership of the estate over to you."

Tension was still there. Her core of steel driving her.

"Define *indefinitely*."

She shrugged. "I don't know. That's the meaning of the word. There's no time frame."

"Not good enough." His gaze intensified. She studied it.

"You want me to promise forever?" she asked, with a definite note of sarcasm.

He continued to speak silently to her.

And his gaze, that feeling he'd brought into her world…they weren't warned off by her steel. Wouldn't shut up and leave her alone.

He did. He wanted forever.

Another vision of Walter's picture room came to her.

She loved that place. Loved the idea of being able to escape into a happy past anytime she wanted to do so.

And she knew.

In the same kind of blink she'd had when she'd had her breakthrough.

She didn't have a choice.

Shaking, in a way as afraid as she'd been as a little girl, lying on a hard road, staring at her mother, she had her clarity. "I can." She looked at him solidly, and then had to blink away tears. "I can promise you forever, West. What can you promise me?"

"That I want to marry you."

She'd known. Deep inside.

And oh God, she was scared to death.

"I want to marry you, too."

He reached for her gently, as she held her arms out to him. Sliding together, they wrapped their arms around each other's backs at exactly the same time. There'd be passion. A ton of it. But in that moment, there was more.

Something stronger than fear. And impervious to death.

He kissed her. And with his lips still touching hers, said, "And I can promise you that no matter what the moments bring, you and I, our hearts, are together forever."

Her tears, and maybe some of his, dripped down to join the kiss. He licked them away. Kissed her again.

And pulled back.

"One other thing," he said, in a voice she recognized. The slightly bossy, a little rude one. One she welcomed.

"What?"

"There's no way in hell you're signing this estate

over to me. It belongs to both of us. You and me, equally. Every single room of it. And I vow that, when you need to travel, I'll go with you."

Smiling, she pulled back an inch. "That's two things," she said, and then her gaze locked on his and she let herself go to him.

To bind herself to him, willingly. Eagerly. She wasn't feeling any urge to travel anywhere. Except upstairs to bed, together.

To make love.

And to sleep.

"I'm guessing that if I'm done running, my wanderlust might disappear, too," she said. "Though travel with you holds exciting possibilities." She'd been alluding to sexual encounters in all kinds of private places, but the words said aloud brought to mind her last family trip. The instant pang was strong. Real.

And when it rose, she acknowledged it and reached for the greatest happiness anyway.

She was done letting fear control her life. Done letting it rob her of a better happiness.

It wasn't going to bind her anymore.

Because after two decades, she'd finally made it home.

* * * * *

Don't miss the online read prequel to
Sierra's Web:

Trusting Her Betrayer

Available at Harlequin.com.

And don't miss the first Sierra's Web book
by Tara Taylor Quinn:

His Lost and Found Family

Available now from
Harlequin Special Edition.

**WE HOPE YOU ENJOYED
THIS BOOK FROM**

Believe in love. Overcome obstacles. Find happiness.

Relate to finding comfort and strength in the
support of loved ones and enjoy the journey
no matter what life throws your way.

6 NEW BOOKS AVAILABLE EVERY MONTH!

#2911 FINDING FORTUNE'S SECRET
The Fortunes of Texas: The Wedding Gift • by Allison Leigh

Stefan Mendoza has found Justine Maloney in Texas nearly a year after their whirlwind Miami romance. Now that he's learned he's a father, he wants to "do the right thing." But for Justine, marriage without love is a deal breaker. And simmering below the surface is a family secret that could change everything for them both—forever...

#2912 BLOOM WHERE YOU'RE PLANTED
The Friendship Chronicles • by Darby Baham

Jennifer Pritchett feels increasingly left behind as her friends move on to the next steps in their lives. As she goes to therapy to figure out how to bloom in her own right, her boyfriend, Nick Carrington, finds himself being the one left behind. Can they each get what they need out of this relationship? Or will the flowers shrivel up before they do?

#2913 THE TRIPLETS' SECRET WISH
Lockharts Lost & Found • by Cathy Gillen Thacker

Emma Lockhart and Tom Reid were each other's one true love—until their dueling ambitions drove them apart. Now Emma has an opportunity that could bring the success she craves. When Tom offers his assistance in exchange for her help with his triplets, Emma can't resist the cowboy's pull on her heart. Maybe her real success lies in taking a chance on happily-ever-after...

#2914 A STARLIGHT SUMMER
Welcome to Starlight • by Michelle Major

When eight-year-old Anna Johnson asked Ella Samuelson for help in fixing up her father with a new wife, Ella only agreed because she knew the child and her father had been through the wringer. Too bad she found herself drawn to the handsome and kind single dad!

#2915 THE LITTLE MATCHMAKER
Top Dog Dude Ranch • by Catherine Mann

Working at the Top Dog Dude Ranch is ideal for contractor Micah Fuller as he learns to parent his newly adopted nephew. But school librarian Susanna Levine's insistence that young Benji needs help reading has Micah overwhelmed. Hiring Susanna as Benji's tutor seems perfect...until Benji starts matchmaking. Micah would give his nephew anything, but getting himself a wife? A feat considering Susanna is adamant about keeping their relationship strictly business.

#2916 LOVE OFF THE LEASH
Furever Yours • by Tara Taylor Quinn

When Pets for Vets volunteer pilot Greg Martin's plane goes down after transporting a dog, coordinator Wendy Alvarez is filled with guilt. She knows a service dog will help, but Greg's just too stubborn. If Wendy can get him to "foster" Jedi, she's certain his life will be forever altered. She just never expected hers to change, as well.

"You still don't belong here." Mariella crossed her arms
over her chest, and Alex commanded himself not to notice
her body, perfect as it was.

"That makes two of us, and yet here we are."

"I was here first," she muttered. He'd heard the argument
before, but it didn't sway him.

"You're not running me off, Mariella. I needed a fresh
start, and this is the place I've picked for my home."

"My plan was to leave the past behind me. You are a
physical reminder of so many mistakes I've made."

"I can't say that upsets me too much," he lied. It didn't
make sense, but he hated that he made her so uncomfortable.
Hated even more that sometimes he'd purposely drive by

her shop to get a glimpse of her through the picture window. Talk about a glutton for punishment.

She let out a low growl. "You are an infuriating man. Stubborn and callous. I don't even know if you have a heart."

"Funny." He kept his voice steady even as memories flooded him, making his head pound. "That's the rationale Amber gave me for why she cheated with your fiancé. My lack of emotions pushed her into his arms. What was his excuse?"

She looked out at the street for nearly a minute, and Alex wondered if she was even going to answer. He followed her gaze to the park across the street, situated in the center of the town. There were kids at the playground and several families walking dogs on the path that circled the perimeter. Magnolia was the perfect place to raise a family.

If a person had the heart to be that kind of a man—the type who married the woman he loved and set out to be a good husband and father. Alex wasn't cut out for a family, but he liked it in the small coastal town just the same.

"I was too committed to my job," she said suddenly and so quietly he almost missed it.

"Ironic since it was your job that introduced him to Amber."

"Yeah." She made a face. "This is what I'm talking about, Alex. A past I don't want to revisit."

"Then stay away from me, Mariella," he advised. "Because I'm not going anywhere."

"Then maybe I will," she said and walked away.

Don't miss
Wedding Season *by Michelle Major,*
available May 2022 wherever
HQN books and ebooks are sold.

HQNBooks.com

PHMMEXP0322